SQUAT

To those who lived in abandoned buildings
and have already climbed the ladder

13-digit ISBN: 978-0-8054-3292-3
10-digit ISBN: 0-8054-3292-2

Published by B & H Publishing Group
Nashville, Tennessee

Dewey Decimal Classification: F
Subject Headings: CITY MISSIONS—FICTION

The characters and the places in this novel are fictitious.

06 07 08 09 10   10 9 8 7 6 5 4 3 2 1

SQUAT

A NOVEL

TAYLOR FIELD

B&H
PUBLISHING GROUP
Nashville, Tennessee

SQUID's NEIGHBORHOOD

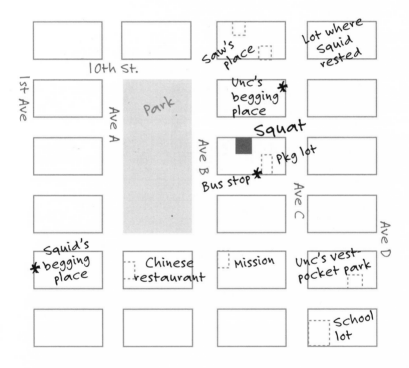

CHAPTER 1

CALMLY, THE GIRL on the sofa reached out and pulled up a flap of skin on the little boy's thin arm. It could have been a gesture of affection. But then she pinched the skin and twisted it. Hard.

"Ouch!" He whipped his pencil in front of her face once, like a club, and then cracked it on her forehead. He pulled the pencil back, ready to strike her again, crouching against the back of the couch like a cornered weasel.

The little girl wrinkled up her round freckled face but did not cry out. She looked toward her mom, who was talking to the receptionist. The boy's mom, seated across the room, didn't look up. She continued to look through the pages of her magazine, snapping each page like a whip.

"You could have put my eye out!" the freckled girl hissed.

The boy rubbed the two blue marks on his arm. He looked her steadily in the eyes and growled.

His mom called him over. "Come sit by me, honey, and stop making so much noise." She patted his hair down in the back and smiled at him. She wore lots of eyeliner and widened her eyes to make even sitting in a waiting room seem like an adventure. "You're such a big man, now," she had said this morning as she combed his hair and helped him put on his best shirt. She was humming "Getting to Know You" even though her voice quivered just a little. She had put a lot of extra perfume and sprays on this morning. She smelled like the women's aisle in a drugstore.

Once the little girl's mom finished with the receptionist and returned to the sofa, the little girl started crying with one soft, unending whine.

The boy rolled his eyes and looked for a book to bury his head in.

"What's wrong, honey?" the mom asked as she swept her little girl up.

"That boy hit me."

A stuffy silence reigned in the waiting room except for the sound of the bubbles in the aquarium above the magazine table. The girl's mother glared at the boy and then at his mother. The boy picked up a children's book with some torn pages and began studying it seriously. His mom hadn't been listening to the girl. She was still snapping through the magazine's pages.

Finally, she threw it down with disgust and looked at her watch again. "I'm going outside to smoke a cigarette, honey," she said, oblivious to the stares of the mother and daughter across the room. She stood up, adjusted her dress with an efficient tug, and stepped outside the office. They gaped at her departure with their mouths open, like two goldfish.

The aquarium continued to gurgle. In the following silence, the little boy became dramatically interested in the book in front of him. It had been pawed over by a lot of children waiting in this doctor's office, and the first few pages had been torn out. The pages that remained had rounded corners and smudges along the edges. The little boy squinted his eyes in exaggerated concentration. He preferred the smudged pictures to the astonished fish eyes of the adult across the room.

He studied a picture of a man who wore a robe down to his ankles. He had a beard and a sad look in his eyes. In front of him was a young man with no beard, lying on a stone with his hands tied. The man with a beard had a knife in his hand and had his hand raised high up as if he were going to stab the boy. Out of a cloud an angel was reaching out to grab the hand of the man. The angel hadn't touched the man yet, but his hand was getting close. The man didn't yet know that the angel was there.

The boy forgot about the girl and her mother. The color of the man's robe was so deep and blue. The angel's wings were more gold than his mother's best bracelet. The boy on the stone had a robe that was silvery-white like clouds. The sun in the background was redder than any sun he had ever seen. It was as red as a hot dog. The little boy felt he was swimming in this world of rich colors and robes, a sleepy world tempered by the sound of the bubbles in the doctor's aquarium. The boy put his finger above the picture book, to the right of the book, and then to the left of the book. "One, two, three. One, two, three. One, two, three," he whispered to himself, touching each of the three points three times.

His mom opened the door and came back in. The summer heat from outside reached in to bathe him in warmth. She shut the door with exasperation. She sat down beside him, reeking of cigarette smoke and hair spray. She adjusted his collar and gave him a nervous smile. "You're such a big man now," she said and patted his hair again.

The boy pointed to the man in the robe in the picture. "Mom, is that boy that man's son?"

"I don't know, honey." She picked up the same magazine again and started ripping through it at lightning speed.

"What's he doing with the knife, Mom?"

His mom gave a half smile and looked at the picture absentmindedly. "He's protecting his boy from someone who might hurt him. Stay still, honey. Why is the doctor making us wait so long? If he doesn't see us by twelve, we'll have to leave. He ought to pay *us* for making us wait."

The boy studied the picture again.

"That's Abraham, stupid," the little girl stage-whispered from across the room.

The boy looked at her and scowled. "Yeah, like you know."

She stuck her tongue out at him and turned it upside down.

His mom backhanded a few more pages, put the magazine down, and looked him in the eyes. She beamed. "Honey, I have a surprise for you. I've been waiting to tell you, and I've been looking for the right moment. I guess no moment is really the right moment. At 12:15 today we are going to see *Sammy* again. He's come back. He'll be waiting for us at our place. Isn't that exciting? Everything will be different. You'll be nice to him, won't you? Honey, don't bite your thumbs, you'll make them bleed again."

The boy wouldn't look at his mom. He stared down at the picture of the man with the knife. Then he looked up at the clock above the receptionist. The little hand was close to the twelve and the big hand was on the eight. He turned the page of the book and another page was torn out. The next page after the torn one had a picture of a man sleeping with his head on a rock. He didn't have a beard and he looked scared. His robe was a dull gray and looked dirty, but in the background, angels were coming up and down out of the sky on a shimmering stairway.

"I want to camp out on my own like this guy does, away from everybody, away from the house," he told his mom.

"That's sweet, honey," she said as she finished the magazine again and looked at her watch.

The little boy's lips moved as he carefully scrutinized the words beneath the picture of the man camping out. His eyes got wider. He traced a word with his finger. He almost forgot where he was. "I want to be like this guy," he whispered.

A man in a suit breezed in and talked to the receptionist. Immediately his mom sat up straighter. The man finished with the receptionist and turned around and looked for a seat. His mom widened her eyes and smiled at the man. He smiled back.

The next page of the book was also torn out. On the following page was the best picture of all. A youth was wearing a beautiful robe with many different stripes of colors. He seemed so happy and looked as though nothing bad would ever happen to him. A man with a white beard was smiling next to him in the picture. The boy stared at the colors in the book for a long time. If he focused his eyes beyond the page, the colors blurred together like rainbow ice cream. Somehow looking at it kept his stomach from hurting so badly.

"Mom, I want a coat like this one."

His mom looked at the picture for a moment. Her tone sounded much more patient with him now that the new man was in the waiting room. "Everybody wants a coat like that, honey. You'll get yours one day."

The little girl stretched her freckled face up as high as she could so she could see the picture. "That's Joseph, you toad," she said hoarsely from across the room. "Don't you ever go to church?"

Her mother pulled her back close to her lap and said, "Hush."

The boy looked at the clock. The big hand was on the nine. "Mom, let's just stay here. It's nice and cool and our air conditioner doesn't work at home. I like looking at the books here. I like the fish. Let's just stay here and not go back home. It's too hot there."

His mom looked at her watch again. "Why are your hands so clammy, sweetie? You're making the book wet. What's wrong with you? Stop biting your thumb or you'll make it bleed right before we see the doctor. Do you want to get me into even more trouble?" She smiled at the man as she got up and walked past him to the receptionist. "Could you tell me how much longer it will be until we can see the doctor? I have another urgent appointment." She conferred with the receptionist for a few minutes in hushed tones.

The boy found an envelope in the back of the book with all the colorful pictures. It had bright green writing on it and a red border. The envelope said you could send off for more books with other stories. The boy looked up at the little girl across the room. She was yanking on her mother's sleeve and whispering something in her ear. She was probably talking about the boy's mom. While making sure the girl was still looking at her own mom, he carefully folded the envelope once and put it in his jean pocket.

The girl was staring insolently at him again. He wanted to do something to the book. He wanted to add a character to protect the boy from the father with the knife. He reached in his other pocket and pulled out half a red crayon. He wanted to draw a picture in the book. He wanted to put someone in there to help that angel keep that boy from getting cut, but he knew that the girl on the opposite couch would never let him get away with drawing in the book. He pulled out his stack of baseball cards as she continued to stare. He carried only Yankees. He pulled his prize Reggie Jackson card from the stack and began to place it in the book but decided against it. He pulled out a relief pitcher, Dick Tidrow. He would be a good enough guard to help the angel. Then he put the card carefully in the page where the sad man was dressed in the long robe and holding the knife. He made sure that the edge of the card was exactly parallel to the edge of the book. He knew the girl was watching him. He closed the book very slowly and with great respect. Very quietly, with just one finger, he touched three sides of the book again, three times. "One, two, three. One, two, three. One, two, three," he said under his breath. He put the book down gently on the table and then put both hands on his stomach and doubled over until his head touched his knees. A groan came out of him before he knew it.

The little girl sneered at him, "You're nuts!" Her mom held her closer and made a shushing sound.

The boy looked at the clock again as his mom plopped down on the sofa with a snort. The big hand was already past the eleven. "Mom, let's stay here. We've already waited a long time. Let's stay."

"Straighten up, sweetie. Why are you bent over? Everything is going to be fine. Soon we will see Sammy and everything will be different. It won't be like last time. You'll see. Everything will be fine." She looked at her watch again then got up to talk to the receptionist. She seemed to be talking faster and faster. Finally she marched back to her son and said firmly, "We're going now. We'll have to come back another day. Let's go, honey. Straighten up and stop frowning."

She grabbed his hand, but he grabbed the arm of the sofa with his other hand. The arm of the sofa had padding on the top, but a metal support on the side. It was just right for grabbing. She pulled and his knuckles whitened. "Come on, sweetie, don't be silly." She smiled at the man and the other mother. She was petite and could not get her son to loosen his grip. He was small for an eleven-year-old, but his grasp was almost as strong as his mother's. She reached to loosen his grip with her hand, but he simply grabbed the arm of the sofa with his other hand.

She smiled sweetly to the man and said, "Would you mind helping me, please?"

He hesitated, got up awkwardly, and began to loosen the grip of the other hand. The aquarium began to rumble like a volcano, and both the receptionist and the other mother stood up. The boy was stretched out like a cartoon as the mother pulled and the man pried his fingers from the sofa. In the middle of the hubbub, the little girl came up to hold his torso, as if to protect him from falling. Where her mother couldn't see, she grabbed the sensitive skin next to his ribs and pulled and twisted at the same time as hard as she could.

In the tussle, the book with the men in robes fell to the floor and the little girl slipped on it. The baseball card slid underneath the sofa. The receptionist picked up the phone to call someone. The other mother grabbed for her daughter. The little boy squealed a high squeal; he was a desperate guinea pig grabbed by many hands.

Finally, the man got both hands loose, and his mom dragged him by the torso and opened the door. He clutched at the frame of the door but couldn't hold on. By that time, some people in white coats came out with the receptionist and shouted as his mom dragged him out to the steaming parking lot. His mother roared back at them with a curse. He cried and whimpered for help as he got one last glimpse of the girl looking out at him from the waiting room window. She stood with her hands on her hips and her tongue sticking out.

Until he ran away from home, a number of years later, the little boy never went back to a doctor.

CHAPTER 2

SQUID HANDLED THE soiled paper gingerly as if it were on fire. One last time he looked at what was written on it. Then with the tips of his fingers, he quickly folded it up and dropped it in the envelope, as though to keep it from burning his skin. The envelope was creased and smudged from being handled. It had a faded red border and green writing on it. Next he placed the envelope into the hole in the exposed wall of bricks a few feet above the floor. His wiry body was crouched next to the window, and he swayed a bit as he made sure the edges of the envelope were parallel to the edges of the brick.

He looked over at Unc swaddled in dirty blankets, making sure he was still asleep. It was not too hot yet. Even in the summer, the inside of the abandoned building smelled damp. In the early morning, it almost felt as though he had air-conditioning. It was as cool as a doctor's office. And much more peaceful. No one was going to take him out of this place. Squid reached out to an old radiator pipe and squeezed it until his fingers hurt, just to prove his point to himself. Then he looked back at the hole in the wall and placed the brick back into its place with slow, quiet concentration. Except for the slight noise of brick on brick, he hardly made a sound.

Glancing out the window for a moment, Squid then looked around for the little chip of brick that was on the floor. He found the red flake, smaller than a dime. Carefully, as if he were setting bait on a spring-loaded trap, Squid placed the sliver of red clay upon the top ridge of the brick he had just placed in the wall. He made sure the chip was in the exact center of the length of the brick. This way he could easily check if anyone had tampered with his hiding place. For someone to read that paper would be blasphemy in Squid's eyes. That person should be struck by fire and roasted. "Roasted on a stick like a hot dog," he whispered out loud through clenched teeth. Squid became very still and looked around again. All he could hear was the hoarse whisper of Unc's steady breathing from the other side of the room.

Then, as he did every morning, he touched the top of the brick, the left side, and the right side, saying, "One, two, three," as he did so. He did it three times quickly: "One, two, three. One, two, three. One, two, three." Again: "One, two, three. One, two, three. One, two, three." Again: "One, two, three. One, two, three. One, two, three." There. He felt better. Twenty-seven times. Three times three times three. He was ready.

Squid looked out the window again. He could squat down comfortably and rest on his heels. With his teeth, he tore the shreds of skin on the side of his thumb. He squinted his eyes to see more clearly. Shafts of morning light were just visible between the buildings. For a moment, Squid noticed that the light reflected red in the windows to the left of him. Red as hot dogs.

Soon Saw would pass by, unaware that his head was about to be cracked open like a cantaloupe dropped on the sidewalk. Squid had to do it. He had no choice. He grabbed the little bat as he crouched. It was an old souvenir bat, given out at some Yankees game. Squid had found it in a garbage can on the street. Its size was diminutive, much smaller than a regulation bat. Still, it was made of wood and had a certain heft and weight. Squid could swing it at frightening speed and to good effect. He was small and wiry, but at twenty years of age, he knew he could hold his own against anybody. His back tightened as he thought about swinging that bat.

Squid was able to look out this back window and see a three-foot space of sidewalk on the next street behind his building. Everything else was blocked by old tenement structures. Squid stared at that three-foot gap with the concentration of a batter watching a pitcher. Soon Saw would pass by on the street, becoming visible for an instant as he returned home from prowling through the night. Squid had seen him pass by at dawn a dozen times. Any minute now. In a flash, Squid's muscles tensed, as if an electric jolt had gone through him. He held himself back. It was just a couple passing by, finishing up their night on the town. Squid could hear the echo of the woman's laughter and the click of her high heels on the sidewalk.

Without moving from his crouched position, Squid stared for a long time at the space. The night had been very humid, but for this brief moment, the air felt almost fresh on Squid's cheeks. He could hear birds singing in the distance at the first light of day. A few sparrows came and landed on the rusted fire escape outside his window. They chattered at Squid like hungry pets. Squid looked hard at the sparrows. They seemed so small and weak. But they were always feisty, always talking, no matter how hot or how cold it was.

Unc said that the male sparrows had a little beard, and the females didn't. When he had it, Squid liked to put some bread out for them and give them a chance to eat before all the pigeons came and took their food away. But today, Squid wouldn't move. He felt like a big cat, ready to pounce. "Get out of my face," he whispered through clenched teeth, trying to sound like a gangster. The sparrows tilted their heads at him for a moment then flew off.

For an instant, Squid looked at the faded white lettering on the little blue bat. He bounced the bat up and down in his hand to test its weight. The Yankee logo was faded but still clear. Squid loved every single Yankee. Someday when he worked up enough courage, he would go to a game. He would wait for Don Mattingly after the game and shake his hand. "I'm your biggest fan!" he'd say, just like that, without any hesitation, without wrapping his hands in his shirt. As he thought about it, Squid put the bat in his left hand and held his right hand out firmly, so that Don would know that he was a regular guy.

He looked back to the three-foot space that showed the street behind him, just as Saw was passing. Almost missed him. But it was Saw, no doubt—the camouflage pants he always wore, the black leather vest with no shirt underneath, the sunglasses. His dark muscular arms blended with the color of the leather. Even in the heat, the black scarf was wrapped around his head. The light flashed on the highly polished army boots, the knife strapped in a sheath to the outside of the calf of his right leg. Squid saw him for just a flicker of a moment. Saw was gone in a flash, but Squid saw him.

Every muscle in his small body tightened for an instant, and then he charged for the door. Like a runner stealing second, he streaked along the hallway to the front section of his own floor, past Unc, past the exposed wood beams with nails sticking out and piles of old bricks. With no electricity in the building, the light was dim, but Squid knew every step. He picked up speed, taking three stairs at a time to the second floor, past the row of dirty mattresses and filthy people lying on them, pieces of paper and lint stuck to their matted hair. Even as he ran, the smell of unwashed bodies and moldy mattresses hit him. Streaking down the first flight of stairs, he stopped for a moment to straddle the banister, to pass the place on the stairway where five steps were gone like missing teeth.

Squid reached out to put his foot on the next slate step that was still there. He missed. His foot went into the empty space, so Squid rolled forward. Turning over once, his feet hit the broken slate of the main floor. The sound of the bat against the stairs made an echo all the way down the empty hall, but in a flash Squid was standing again.

Squid raced down the darkened hallway on the main floor, jumping over a crumpled body extending into the hall from a doorway. Squid sprinted to the front door. A chain extended out from the hole where the lock used to be. The hallway echoed with the sound of his hands slapping against the door to stop his motion. The chain was padlocked, so he turned to the room to the right, where a portion of the concrete brick had been knocked out of a sealed-up window. Protecting the bat, he scrambled through the opening, rage roaring through his body like a subway train. Saw was much bigger than he was, but that didn't matter now.

When his feet hit the sidewalk, he balanced his bat like a weapon and charged toward the corner. Saw would have made a right turn at the corner a block away to return home. When Squid turned this corner, he should run right into him. One swift whack to the head, maybe two, before Saw could reach his knife, and it would be all over. Saw would never be fast enough to lift that knife to strike. Everything would be all right again. Squid had to do it. He turned the corner and raised his bat in the air.

Nothing. No one was there. Squid stood on the sidewalk and stared at an empty street. No one was watching.

This would have been perfect. Even if someone were looking out the window of one of these abandoned buildings, chances were they weren't the type to call the police. Squid stood alone on the sidewalk with his little blue bat, ready to strike.

Where could Saw have gone? He must have been going home. He should have turned left at the corner. Squid wanted to sprint to the next corner to look down the street, but his legs wouldn't move. Squid waited a moment. Surely Saw had enough time to get to the corner by now. Still nothing. What could Saw be doing? Maybe he went to the store. Or maybe he stopped to make some last unknown visit. Was he working on some attack plan related to Squid? Did Squid just dream that he saw him for that fraction of a second between two buildings? Or perhaps Saw was crouched next to the corner building right now, waiting for Squid to walk by, so that Saw could ambush him before the light was full. Squid knew he should race to the corner right now, but fear bolted his feet to the street. Saw was no fool. Squid could almost see Saw, knife in hand, crouched beside the wall of the building; he could almost sense him with that big knife balanced easily in his hand.

Squid stood in the middle of the street, the avenging blue bat dangling at his side. He felt paralyzed. In a rush, two strong arms grabbed him in a bear hug from behind and squeezed like a python.

A current of fear jolted through Squid's body and constricted his throat. Squid opened his mouth to scream, but nothing came out. The arms lifted Squid off the ground, squeezing harder and harder. Squid couldn't breathe and began to feel a light-headed despair. His little bat hit the sidewalk. He was on the verge of blacking out. Squid's life did not pass before his eyes. But his last weak thought, sifting into his consciousness as if from a radio with the volume turned down very low, was *Now I will never go to a Yankees game with her.*

The arms dropped him to the ground, released him, and pushed him away in one quick motion. Squid staggered and spun around, reaching for his bat. "Ahh man, ahh man." Squid sucked in air. "Bonehead, you scared the life out of me. I can't breathe. I gotta sit down. I need to see a doctor."

Bonehead held his ample stomach and bent over laughing. He clapped his dirty hands and rubbed them through his white hair, looking very pleased. "Whadja think, whadja think," he chuckled in a hoarse, slurred voice. Squid couldn't understand what Bonehead said half the time, but he endured him in the park because Squid knew he was a bonehead, slow or retarded or something.

"Leave me alone, Bonehead. I've got big problems today. Big problems."

Bonehead just kept laughing and said, "Whadja think," one more time.

"What happened to your belt, Bonehead?" Bonehead had a rope tied around his waist to hold up his pants. Bonehead's pants were once blue, but now they looked black and shiny, as if covered with grease.

Bonehead mumbled, "Haddachangewhatyagothere," but Squid couldn't understand. Bonehead was still laughing.

"Bonehead, you don't even have a belt anymore. You look like something out of the funny papers." Squid began to feel a little stronger. Squid held his bat with one hand and grabbed Bonehead's shirt and twisted it with his other hand. He yanked Bonehead toward him. "If you ever scare me like that again, I'm going to break your fingers with this bat," Squid snarled.

He pushed Bonehead away and rolled his own hand up into his shirt. He could never understand how Bonehead lived. He couldn't figure how in the world Bonehead took care of himself.

"When did you last eat, you idiot?" Squid reached in his pocket and found three quarters. "Here, Bonehead, buy yourself a bagel or something. You should be proud of yourself. You've already given me a total heart attack. You've made me lose my appetite for a month. Go ahead and take this—I can't use it. I can't eat now. I'll probably starve to death." Bonehead took the money, still chuckling.

Squid looked around one more time for Saw. "I've got to talk to Unc," Squid said to no one. "Now don't follow me, Bonehead." He left Bonehead wheezing and chuckling in the middle of the street.

Squid retraced his steps back to the abandoned building he called home. He walked gingerly around a stoop and then a pile of trash where someone could be hiding. It was going to be a hot day. The trash smelled like urine and rotten eggs and already had some fat flies hovering over it. Squid took the bottom of his shirt and wiped the sweat off his stomach. He looked up and saw a haze around the streetlights that had not been turned off yet. It was still early in the morning, but already it was getting hard to breathe.

Water poured in a steady stream out of the fire hydrant on the street. Someone Squid did not know was washing his underwear in the flow. He had nothing on. "What do you want me to do, call the police?" Squid muttered under his breath as he passed the naked man. But people didn't call the police when they got robbed or beat up here. If something happened in their squat, they took care of it themselves. *That's what the Lower East Side is like now*, Squid mused. Things had changed. The old Ukrainian guys who drink in the park would tell Squid that things were really nice here once. But not now, not in the late eighties, especially for people who "squatted" in an empty building.

Every squatter is illegally trespassing. Squatters are living on city-owned property without permission, so calling the police is out of the question. The exposed man crouched next to the stream and twisted the water out of his shorts. He didn't even look at Squid. Squid passed by suspiciously and said under his breath, "One, two, three."

He looked up at his own building. Some of the windows were covered with old plywood. The windows on the main floor were sealed with concrete blocks. Old wood beams stuck out from an open upper window. Squid's building looked like a homeless person who had put his outfit together from all kinds of patches and sources.

Sometime before Squid had moved into the building, someone had taken a sledgehammer and smashed open the cement blocks the city had used to seal up the front-door opening. A door frame and metal door had been salvaged from a dumpster somewhere and installed, inaugurating one more "squat," another building taken over by force from the city.

Squats were all over the place in this neighborhood. Some streets seemed like they were just a whole row of squats. The industrious person who installed the door at Squid's place was long gone. Squid knew of no one in the building now who was capable of doing such a thing. Yet the chain that looped through a hole next to the frame and through the hole in the door was sometimes locked by somebody, as it was now. The building was covered with graffiti. A new message in red spray paint was on the door: *Death to Yuppies.*

Squid climbed through the opening in the window next to the door, clenching his bat. The hallway was still cool and damp. He stopped for a moment to enjoy the coolness on his skin. He stepped much more quietly over the motionless body still extending out of the doorway into the hall. It was just a junkie who was sleeping. Squid didn't know who it was. Slowly he climbed the stairs then straddled the banister where the missing steps were.

Several times he stopped, just to listen. The people on the dirty mattresses had not moved. He could hear the faint snores and regular breathing. Squid snorted at the body odor and moldy bedding and dirty clothes. A sewage smell lurked in the background. Everybody was supposed to use a bucket with a top for a toilet—that was a rule for the squat. But some of these people on the second floor were so far gone they didn't care what they did.

He remembered when he was eleven years old and had a clean toilet that flushed, a shower, and a washer and dryer. Even if his car didn't have air-conditioning, the houses he stayed in often did. He remembered clean clothes and his mom patting down his combed hair and singing to him. Things that seemed so familiar then—a phone, a refrigerator, a television—seemed impossible now. Now he lived in a place with no electricity, no plumbing, and in some places, no windows. "So what," he said under his breath.

On the third floor, Unc hadn't moved. Fifteen blankets and sheets swirled around Unc's body like waves. Books and clothes and papers were scattered all over Unc's side of the room. Nothing was scattered on Squid's side of the room. The mattress, his old suitcase, his other pair of sneakers were all placed in symmetrical positions, each thing parallel to the rest of the items on his side. His extra pair of sneakers was centered perfectly in the middle of his space.

"Wake up, Unc, wake up." Squid pulled a dirty sheet out from under him. Unc rolled over involuntarily. "Wake up, Unc. How can you breathe with all these blankets around? Unc, I am in deep, deep trouble. You got to talk to me, Unc. You got to talk to me right away."

Squid pulled the blanket up until Unc rolled all the way over to the wall. Unc sighed, rubbed his big hands over his moustache, and slowly tried to sit up. "Please bring me a bottle," Unc croaked. Unc's thinning hair was standing straight up. With slow care, he ran his fingers through the thickest part.

"There's nothing left to drink, Unc, I've checked. Please, please talk to me—I am in so, so much trouble." Squid was squatting next to Unc now. Unc, as big as a walrus, succeeded in sitting up.

"Fortitude, fortitude," Unc intoned. "Fortitude will always lead to pulchritude." He was much older than Squid, but it was hard to tell how much older. His skin had that dark, creased, leathery look of someone who had drunk a lot, smoked a lot, and slept outside a lot. Slowly Unc pulled a yellowed bed sheet around his body. He almost always had a blanket or sheet wrapped around him, even in the hottest parts of summer. He wore it when he was sitting inside, reading and drinking, or when he was sitting outside reading, drinking, and begging.

Unc sat up cross-legged, robed in the sheet. He had missed a whole section of his hair, which was still sticking straight up. Squid rubbed his eyes and waited. He looked at Unc's lopsided Mohawk and decided not to mention it. He knew it would take awhile for Unc to wake up entirely.

"So, what is happening?" Unc finally asked in his bass voice. "You look as calm and relaxed as someone awaiting a lobotomy." He rubbed his eyes and felt around in the blankets for a bottle.

"Oh, Unc, I did such a stupid, stupid thing." Squid bit again at the shreds of skin on the side of his thumb. Then he hid his hands under his shirt. Unc sat as still as a tribal chief and didn't speak. Squid plunged ahead. "You see, I met Saw on the street yesterday."

Unc rubbed his scalp, missing the sticking-up hair. "You're hanging out with Saw now?"

"No, no, but anyway, I said I had this great weed, which I did. But you see I'd smoked it all—it really calmed me down—and I didn't have any left. But I *said* I had some left. I don't know why I said that—Saw makes me nervous. I guess I wanted to impress him. I guess I wanted him to think I had connections. I guess I wanted him to think I could score drugs like he could. I don't know. I have no idea what I was thinking, really. Then Saw gets up real close and all intimidating and says he wants some. You probably know what happened to me then. I couldn't speak. My throat froze up. Saw gave me a hundred dollars to get him some. And I just took the money."

At this point, Unc groaned and rubbed his hands through his hair again, but Squid kept talking. "I was supposed to bring it to him yesterday afternoon. Now he's attacking me in the neighborhood. He's saying I robbed and cheated him. How dare he disrespect me, Unc. My good name is all I have left among my friends." Squid's body stiffened and he tried to sneer like a gangster. "I should kill Saw for that. Or at least give him a concussion. Oh, Unc, I'm in such big trouble." Squid unwrapped his hand from his shirt and bit down hard on the side of his thumb. "I don't get my disability check until next week."

Unc squinted at the sunlight. "This is not a sickness unto death. Have you got his money with you?" Unc's gravity-defying hair glowed in the sunlight now coming through the window.

"Now don't go crazy on me, Unc, I can't handle it. You see, well . . . I don't have it anymore."

Unc groaned again and rubbed his bushy moustache.

"I bought a gift for someone — a Yankees Deluxe Album for $89.50. It was very important."

"Who in Gehenna, and I do mean in *Gehenna*, did you buy a book for?" Squid looked at Unc with a startled expression. He guessed that Gehenna must mean hell. Unc did not approve of cursing unless you could make it sound like Shakespeare or some poet from hundreds of years ago. He didn't allow Squid or Bonehead to curse in his presence.

"Just somebody." Squid shifted his weight.

Unc searched Squid's face. Squid sat there defensively and said nothing. He could talk nonstop, but he never talked about his family or where he came from. Not with anybody. In an unguarded moment once, he told Unc his mother was white and he had no idea who his father was. Squid's skin was dark.

He looked so tightly wired there in front of Unc, so pleading, like a squirrel or a chipmunk, hungry for any protection or help.

"I know I messed up, Unc, but it was really, really important and I just had to do it and it didn't matter to me what happened later. Haven't you ever had a time when something inside your chest kept getting bigger and bigger and you just had to do something, even if it wasn't smart, and besides it was something good anyway? That's all I know and that's all I can say right now."

Unc sighed and looked at the ceiling. "Ah, man is a giddy thing . . . that's how Shakespeare said it. How could anyone explain the reason we do things? The heart has reasons that reason will never know. Look, grandson." Unc used *grandson* when he was feeling most protective. "There are many people in the park that talk trash. They will threaten you, act like they are going to fight, posture, pull a knife out, even a gun. But they will do nothing. It's just a pose. Still, it's wise to avoid them."

Squid looked at Unc hopefully. "I know that, Unc."

"On the other hand," Unc continued hoarsely, "Saw . . . is usually in jail. When he's out, he's doing something crazy. He doesn't care. As much as I hate incarceration, this neighborhood is a better place when he is a resident of our wonderful penal system. Remember that guy in the park with the scar from the bottom of his neck up to his forehead? Saw did that, or at least he said he did it." Unc's voice got lower and lower as he talked, until Squid had to lean forward on his haunches to hear him. "Saw just wanted to scare him. You can't predict what Saw might do."

Squid dropped his head and sprawled out on the floor. He knocked over a pile of books. Unc had those books everywhere. Squid put his head in his arms and moaned. "I'm dead. This is the end." Squid writhed around on the floor, pushing books and blankets around with his arms and legs. "Look at my thumbs, Unc, I'm a mess. I belong under a doctor's care, Unc, not out here on the street. Do you think I could go to a hospital or a clinic or something and hide in the waiting room all day?"

"I doubt that our esteemed medical profession could handle the exigencies of your challenge today, grandson. People on the street try to find protection in a waiting room all the time. In your state, you'd be asked to leave within ten minutes." Unc pulled a book out of the chaos and wiped the smudges off the cover.

Squid rolled his hands up into his shirt. "Someone's going to die today. Either I'm going to kill myself or get killed or I'll kill him. Saw doesn't know how crazy I can get. I'll take him out. Oh, this is the worst day of my life."

"All is not lost, grandson. This is what you need to do. You see, Saw is going to have to do something bad to you. Even if he were a nice gentleman, he would have to do something bad to you. Saw isn't really stupid. He's criminally psychotic, but he's not stupid. He's like a lot of other people around here. He works just as hard to achieve his goals as an investment banker downtown. Saw just uses different means to do it."

Unc rubbed his moustache and looked out the window. "You've got to look at this from Saw's perspective. You have to think like a sociologist. His good name, or rather *bad* name, is the only tool of his business, whatever business that may be this week. If someone has cheated him—and believe me, Squid, you have cheated him—he has to hurt you. His reputation is his essence. If *you* can cheat him and get away with it, then anyone can cheat him. And, you see, Saw is not a nice gentleman.

You are like a little tree branch to him. He is like," and Unc was relishing his words, "he is like the grinder in a lumber yard."

Squid sat up on the floor and wove his legs together. "So what do I do, Unc?"

Unc put his hands together, fingertips to fingertips, like a lawyer advising his client. "It's easy. You leave. You get on a subway and go anywhere. You take a PATH train. You go to the bus station. You go to Jones Beach and sleep under a bridge. You just get out of here as fast as you can. Come back in a week and I will tell you what is going on."

Squid unwrapped his legs and rolled his hands in his shirt very tightly. "I'm not doing that, Unc."

Unc was silent, awaiting an explanation.

"I'm not leaving until after tomorrow morning. I've got to be here at four in the morning."

Unc took a deep breath and let out a sigh. "Look, Squid, life decisions have never been your strong point, nor mine. But this is not a game. What have you got to do at four in the morning that is worth your shredded flesh?"

Squid bit his thumb and said through his teeth, "Just something important."

Unc looked at Squid with a bemused smile. Then he looked out the window at the morning light. "I hope you change your mind. The sooner, the better. At any rate, I would call this a big day for you. It may be the most significant day of your short life."

"Unc, I don't want a long life. But I just don't want to get cut up in some empty lot somewhere. Won't you help me? Won't you stay with me through this day?"

Unc finished wiping off the dirty paperback he had pulled from the scattered books. It had a faded picture of a Chinese warrior on the front. "Twenty-five-hundred years ago Sun Tzu said that all warfare is based on deception. You'll have to think like a warrior today."

"What does that mean?" Squid leaned on his side and screwed up his face at Unc.

"Act as a warrior would act. Do the unexpected. Attack when he thinks you'll run. Run when he thinks you'll attack. Move when he thinks you'll sleep. Sleep when he thinks you'll move. No problem. Does he know where you live?" The building suddenly seemed very quiet.

"Yes, he knows where I live. Everyone knows where I live, Unc. I told him where I live yesterday after he gave me the money. I don't know why I did that. After Saw gave me the money, I found my voice again, but I don't know what I was talking about. He was just standing closer and closer to me, and I got freakier and freakier and started talking as fast as I could. You know how I get when I'm nervous. Either I can't talk at all or I talk like a maniac."

Unc jerked like a fish on a hook. He bolted to his feet with astonishing speed. His Mohawk stood at attention. "I think it's time for us to go." He looked around for his shoes. With surprising speed, he scooped up a small bottle under a blanket and started shuffling rapidly through his paperbacks.

A sharp crack rang out from the top of the stairs and reverberated through the room like an explosion. In the spirit of the warrior, Squid did the unexpected. He curled up in a fetal position and counted to three rapidly. Nine times in a row.

CHAPTER 3

"WHADJA THINK?" BONEHEAD stood at the door of Squid's room. In one hand he held an old plastic mop handle, and in the other, the tail of a small lifeless rat. As he entered the room and looked around, he made some guttural noises, from which Squid could make out the phrase, "Got'em."

"Bonehead, are you trying to kill me today?" Squid spread out on the floor and draped his forearm over his forehead. "If you want to whack rats, could you do it somewhere else so you don't scare the whiz out of me?"

Bonehead walked into the empty room in the front of the building and tossed the rat out the window.

"No, Bonehead," Squid groaned. "Oh, great. Now you've probably scared the breakfast out of someone walking on the sidewalk. Can you imagine walking along the sidewalk, feeling fine, and having a dead rat land on top of your head?" Bonehead grinned.

Unc came out from a closet with no door and calmly sat down among his books. He was sitting in a soup of dirty blankets and old paperbacks. He wrapped a sheet around himself and picked up a paperback and began to read it. Unc read everything. His tastes were democratic—Dante, Homer, Shakespeare, child pornography, murder mysteries, cheap science fiction.

Squid did not like what was happening. This was the first time Bonehead had ever been in Squid's room. Usually Bonehead was just pestering and irritating Squid in the park. That was bad enough. Yet here was Bonehead roaming around Squid's room, no less, throwing rats out the window, muttering to himself, poking around.

Bonehead went to look out the back window. Squid looked around and grabbed his Yankees bat. Bonehead was getting closer to the wall with the loose brick. If Bonehead got any closer, Squid would break his arm. Squid got up in a squatting position and held the bat, ready to spring.

Unc didn't notice. "Squid is in trouble, Bonehead." He put down his book. Squid glanced over at Unc for a moment then turned back to Bonehead. Bonehead shuffled over to Unc's swamp of blankets, and Squid relaxed a bit. "You're going to have to stay with him all the time," Unc said, smirking. His thin hair was still standing straight up. "He needs a bodyguard. You're going to have to stick to him like glue today."

"No, no, Bonehead, he's just kidding. You don't have to worry about me." The rage began to rise up in Squid's throat again. This time he was mad at both Bonehead and Unc.

"Whatzad?" Bonehead pointed to an index card that was dangling from a nail next to Unc's books.

"Oh, that card is just for you, Bonehead." Unc deepened his voice with Shakespearean drama. "It says, 'What is the knocking? / What is the knocking at the door in the night? / It is somebody wants to do us harm. / No, no it is the three strange angels. / Admit them, admit them.'"

Unc quoted it from memory. "That's from D. H. Lawrence," he added, "one of our great poets." Unc was always writing out quotes and putting them on the wall. He called himself a wordsmith. Sometimes he gave an index card to Squid with some quote or poem on it. Half the time, Squid couldn't understand it. The card Unc just quoted was a new one.

"Wow," Squid said, "that's sounds kind of religious."

"Well, maybe I am religious in some kind of Zen-pantheistic-Hindu-Native-American way."

"Unc, are you really part Cherokee?"

Unc blew air out his mouth with derisive humor. "Naw, I just said so in that argument with that missionary." Unc placed his fingertips together again. "Now, as you know, Squid, we cannot stay here. Our first test today as warriors found you rolled up in a ball on the floor and me hiding in the closet. If Bonehead could get in here so easily, so could anyone else. We are subject to ambush here. We need to think more strategically and we need to keep moving. Let's leave as a threesome and do something I don't normally do. Let's get some free breakfast at the mission."

Squid's face turned red. "Let me change clothes," he said. "Bonehead, I don't want you roaming around. You stay over here with the books. Unc, if he comes close to my

stuff, tell me, 'cause I am going to break his arm, I swear."
Squid found the least worn of his shirts, folded in a neat
pile in a corner, and took it to the room that used to be a
bathroom.

These days Squid usually did not wash his clothes.
He just wore them until they were unusable and got some
more at one of the churches or bought them used on the
street from someone who had taken them from a church.
He could usually buy something for some pocket change.
Squid picked up the Yankees bat and shook it at Bonehead.
He also scooped up some string from the floor on Unc's side
and put it into his pocket.

The bathroom still had a door, but he couldn't shut
it because then he would be standing in the dark. He left
the door open, but Unc and Bonehead could not see him.
Squid looked at the room for a moment. He remembered
having a real bathroom when he was younger, when the fan
came on when you turned on the lights. He remembered
clean towels and running water. He knew how convenient
a toilet was, rather than using a plastic spackling bucket
with a snap-on top. Now he kept the bucket in the corner
until he had to go dump it late at night in the vacant lot
next door. In this bathroom, there was only a hole where
the toilet used to be. The old cast-iron bathtub was broken
in two. It was still the most private place he had. First he
put on the shirt that was less smelly and folded the other
one up neatly. Then he carefully tied the string around the
handle of the bat.

"Hurry up, Squid. Bonehead is looking for more rats."

Squid tied the other end of the string to the belt loop closest to his left hip. He dropped the small bat inside his baggy pant leg. It wasn't an ideal solution. If he were in a rush, he would probably have to break the string, but somehow he felt better. His pants were so loose that when he stood straight, the bat was not visible. Every time he bent his leg, however, the edge of the bat was visible below the knee.

A shard of a mirror still hung from the wall. Squid patted his head repeatedly, almost desperately, trying to get his short hair into shape.

"Hurry up, Squid!" Unc called out. "Our position is vulnerable and exposed. In colloquial terms, we are sitting ducks here."

Squid fussed with his hair awhile longer and then came out of the bathroom.

"The warrior emerges," Unc proclaimed. "Let's go, Sir Launcelot. I can only guess what weapon you have concealed beneath your armor."

"Don't tease me today, Unc. Bonehead, stop pacing. You're driving me nuts."

As usual, Unc wrapped himself in a sheet. He had a paperback book with the word *Niebuhr* on it. Squid watched him slip a small bottle into his front pocket also. Unc already smelled more like alcohol. Squid decided not to tell him yet about his spectacular Mohawk hair-do. Perhaps at breakfast.

Squid herded Bonehead and Unc toward the stairs. Squid went back to the bathroom, looked at his hair one more time, and pulled a plastic bag out from behind the broken bathtub. In contrast to the rest of the surroundings, the bag was new and fresh and had the Yankees insignia on it.

Squid tried to stick the bag under his shirt, but after a moment, he gave up and simply placed it under his arm.

Everyone was still sleeping on the second floor, and Squid had to tell Bonehead to shut up several times. As always, Unc had a little trouble getting out the side window.

The threesome walked along the sidewalk. Unc wore his sheet, looking like Socrates with skyscraper hair. Bonehead was filthy with a rope for a belt. He was using his mop handle as a walking stick. Squid looked the most normal with his plastic bag under his arm. Still, he walked a bit stiffly on one leg, like a pirate. A philosopher, a dirty Franciscan, and a buccaneer. In some neighborhoods, they would have attracted attention. But not in this one.

———

Already it was very humid. Squid was sweating. Windows were open in tenement buildings, and several large women, all Hispanic on this block, were leaning out the windows and watching the people who passed by on the street. Each of them had a pillow underneath her elbow. When any one of them saw someone they knew, they would raise their head slightly in acknowledgment. Squid didn't know their names, but they knew him. They knew everyone on the street, and they knew when a new person came on the street.

Squid knew a lot of people the three passed, but he didn't know their names. One man passed, pushing a shopping cart with bottles in it. Squid saw him every day, but the man always looked straight ahead and gave Squid no acknowledgment. That's what he liked about the city—no matter what he looked like or what he did, no one paid him any attention. No one cared at all.

Unc watched the man with the shopping cart pass by. It often seemed as though Unc were reading his thoughts. "*Magna civitas, magna solitudo,*" Unc proclaimed officiously.

"What's that mean?" Squid asked. Squid kept scanning places ahead of him where someone could jump out and ambush him. He felt better that he was with two other people and that other people were on the street with him. Like an animal in a herd, he knew he was safer here than anywhere that was lonely or dark. That was key in this neighborhood—having other people around as witnesses in case of attack . . . or being totally invisible.

"A great city is great solitude," Unc said. "It is an old Roman saying. You and I, my friend, are left alone in this neighborhood to follow our own particular peccadillos."

"Well, there are certainly a lot of them to pick from."

"Do you know why a lot of people like that guy with the shopping cart are on the street in this neighborhood, Squid? Because they are not very good secretaries. They are not the type of people who say, 'OK, it's nine o'clock. I've got to go see my caseworker. It's ten o'clock, time to stand in line for admission to rehab. Oh, it's noon. I need to fill out my form to check on my section-eight housing.

I need to keep all my papers for the review of my sanity at Bellevue tomorrow.' These people, Squid, just don't think like that. They are not good at shuffling schedules and keeping a string of appointments. Sadly, that's not what this age demands of them. They might have been great in another time. Attila the Hun may not have been good at shuffling papers and keeping a string of appointments either. Who knows? However, these people here, like that guy, perhaps they have other skills. They might be good at catching someone like you on a day when you are in trouble, getting you in a corner somewhere for fifteen minutes or so."

"Don't talk like that, Unc. You know it freaks me out, and I know you are just messing with my mind. Guys like that wouldn't hurt a fly. They're too zoned out to know which end of their shopping cart is the front. They're like Bonehead—spacey. Hey, Ratchet, what's happening?"

Ratchet had long blond hair and a severe Van Dyck beard. He looked a little bit like Custer. He wore cowboy boots and had a python snake draped around his arm as he sauntered down the sidewalk.

"Not much, just taking Snappy for a walk," he drawled. His Texan accent was strong. His father had been a sheriff in some small town there. "I'm beat, man, I haven't been to sleep yet." Ratchet lived in a squat a few blocks away, but the way he talked sounded like he lived on a ranch somewhere. "Unc, do you know your hair is standing straight up, man? You look like some kind of wasted punk, man."

Unc touched the top of his head gravely, but his hand missed his hair.

"Why don't you go eat breakfast with us, man?" Squid asked. Bonehead had walked ahead of them. Bonehead picked up a piece of gravel, pitched it straight up into the air, and took a swing at it with his mop handle. He hit it squarely and the small stone shot down the block. It hit the bumper of a car with a loud *ping*. "Stop that, you bonehead!" Squid shouted.

"Nah," Ratchet said, shifting Snappy to the other arm. "I got to get some sleep. I gotta take care of Snappy here. Isn't that right, Snappy?" He stroked Snappy's side. Snappy didn't move at all to acknowledge the caress. "By the way," he said, looking at Squid, "Saw is looking for you."

Squid's eyes got larger, as if Snappy were wrapped around his neck. Unc stepped in and took over the conversation. "When did you see him last?"

"He was in the park this morning looking for Squid. That guy is always hunting for somebody."

"Well, we're going to keep moving," Unc said, shepherding Squid forward. "See you."

Unc and Squid walked faster and caught up with Bonehead, who swung his mop handle at a large horsefly flying above a trash can. Bonehead killed the fly on the first swing.

Unc kept pushing Squid forward. Squid began to bite feverishly on the edge of his thumb. "Come on, Squid. Into the mouth of the wolf. That's what opera singers say in Italy before they go onstage. Remember, this is your significant day. This day promises to present some high drama. And I am with you, at least for now."

Squid tapped the bat on the inside of his pants and marched forward more resolutely, feeling more like a pirate all the time.

"How often do you go to the mission to eat breakfast these days?" Unc asked.

"Not too often. 'I'm usually asleep now, at least lately. I usually go to the mission later."

"Good. Remember to go where you usually don't go today and do what you usually don't do. Sun Tzu's advice still holds. Deception is the key to all warfare. Let's keep Saw off balance. What are they serving for breakfast these days?"

Bonehead lagged behind and hit his mop handle on a fire hydrant. Squid whirled around as if he had been shot. Then he shook his head and answered Unc. "Usually oatmeal or cereal and orange juice and coffee. The oatmeal tastes like plaster." Squid began to pat his hair again. He knew that she might be there at the breakfast. As much as Squid liked to talk, he had never said a word about her to Unc. Yet Unc had been watching him with unusual interest the last few days. "How does my breath smell, Unc? I want to get some gum or something. You don't have any, do you?"

Unc shrugged his shoulders and Squid slipped into a corner store. He was ashamed to go into many of the stores, even in this neighborhood, but this store was seedy enough that Squid was not embarrassed. "You want a piece?" Squid offered some gum to Unc when he returned. Bonehead crowded in behind Squid. "OK, you can have some too, you bonehead." Squid began to chew furiously. "How do I look, Unc. Do you think I look presentable?"

"'Presentable' is a relative term, Squid, but yes, you look fine."

Squid shifted his Yankees bag to the other hand and tried to pat the stiff hair he hadn't been able to reach. "Unc, I'm really nervous."

"You've got a lot to be nervous about." Unc looked at him closely. "Now if the line is too long, we can't stay." They turned the corner and saw the mission. It was on the first floor of an old building in some disrepair. People were standing in line in front of the building, waiting to get in. A sign written on poster paper said *Everything for everybody.*

Unc looked at the sign and said, "Oh, what a promise. They must have some new volunteers. Perhaps they have some real fundamentalists in the group." Unc looked at Squid with one eyebrow raised. "They're my specialty, you know."

The line was not too long, so they stood at the end. The line was the usual assortment of people—black, white, Hispanic, men, women, a few children with bedraggled moms, some adults who were very old and some in their twenties. Everyone's clothes looked dirty and drab. Anything white looked yellow and sweat-stained in the sun. A couple of teenage punk rocker-types, covered in drooping chains, were there for breakfast too. One had a small screwdriver piercing his ear. Despite the dissimilarities, there was a striking sameness to the people in the line. The humidity was oppressive, and everyone's shoulders were sagging. No one was talking; everyone was looking down at the ground. No one even had the energy to say, "Quit shoving." Everyone's skin, like their clothes, seemed damp, soiled, and limp. No one was energetic or happy. No one but Squid.

Squid couldn't keep himself from getting excited. He might see her inside the mission. She might be there. He would be right there in the same room with her. If she were inside, it would feel like Christmas and his birthday—all rolled up into one bright moment. He began to think of things he could say. How could he get her attention? Perhaps there was something that could make her laugh. He mentally rehearsed how he might make his presentation to her. How could he make the book sound like nothing, yet let her know how important it was to him? How could he let her know how he had sacrificed for that gift, how he might get killed for that gift? How could he do that but also let her know that it was no big deal to him? How could he say all that and yet not betray the hurricane of emotions inside himself to her or anyone else around? Squid bit hard on the side of his thumb, looked at it, and wrapped his hand up in the bottom of his T-shirt.

Unc looked at Squid shifting around as they waited in line. "Do you need to take a pee, Squid? What's wrong with you? Saw's not going to be inside at this time of day."

"Oh, yeah," Larry said. He was standing in line in front of Unc and heard Unc talking. Larry's clothes were unexceptional, but he had some spectacular hats. On this humid day, he wore a sagging sombrero, though he looked more like he was from the Caribbean than Mexico.

Larry looked at Squid. "Saw is looking for you. I saw him on Tenth Street this morning. What did you do to him, man?"

"How long ago was that?" Unc acted nonchalant.

"A couple of hours ago."

Unc put his hand on Squid's shoulder. "Not to worry."

Squid nodded but didn't care. He would fight a hundred Saws, a thousand, if he had a chance to see her. He couldn't help but feel lighthearted.

CHAPTER 4

THE INSIDE OF the mission was one large room with an open window to the kitchen on one side. Rows of old tables with benches filled the room. It looked a little like Squid's old middle school cafeteria, only dirtier and more used. Squid, Unc, and Bonehead moved through the line and got some oatmeal, orange juice, and toast. No one was talking. It was too hot inside. A few old window fans droned away. Squid was chewing feverishly on his gum and looking around the room.

The three sat down on a bench in a row on the same side of the table, working on their food in silence.

"Try not to be so loud!" A tall young woman sat down on a bench opposite them. She had freckles and blue eyes, and at the end of her sentence, she looked cross-eyed at Squid to let him know that he was in on the joke. She wiped a strand of her brown hair out of her mouth.

Everyone sitting in range of the voice lit up, even Unc. "Rachel! Come to cause trouble among the peons again! Sit down."

"I don't know what a pee-on is, but if it's something that happened at breakfast, I had nothing to do with it." Rachel's mouth was serious, but her eyes laughed as she spoke. She had a way of saying things that always included everyone in earshot in the tease. She had a piece of toast in her hand and took a bite.

Squid could not speak. Rachel usually floated through the room at mealtime as she worked, laughing or sharing a tease with different people at different tables. She had never sat down at his table before. Bonehead was beaming at their good fortune and responded by shoveling more oatmeal into his mouth. Squid pretended to put a little bit of oatmeal in his mouth. He kept the gum between his teeth and his cheek, just in case his breath was as bad as he feared.

Rachel turned to Squid again and wrinkled her nose. "How can you stand to eat that stuff, Squid? It tastes like old soap." Again, Squid could not speak. Everything she did and said seemed so, so cute. He couldn't describe it.

Finally he was able to croak, "No, it tastes like plaster!" He grinned a half grin, trying to keep the gum securely inside his mouth.

"That's it! Soapy plaster. That's what it tastes like." She turned her glow to Bonehead. "Only Bonehead could make this food look delicious. I don't know how you do it, Bonehead. You ought to be on TV selling food. You'd make a million." Bonehead's grin almost touched his ears, and a little oatmeal came out between his teeth.

"To what can we attribute the honor of your presence

at our table?" Even Unc could not hide his pleasure. "Have you laid aside your servant's towel?"

Rachel giggled. "No, we have a new volunteer who is taking my place with the silverware."

Unc rubbed his hands together. "Ah, fresh meat!" He winked at Rachel.

"Oh, I think this one can handle anything you can dish out." Rachel turned around and looked at the area where some volunteers were working.

The conversation stopped for a moment as she turned, and Squid saw his chance. "Do you like baseball, Rachel?"

Rachel turned to him with a diplomatic tone. "Yeah, it's OK."

Squid plowed right in. "I got something for you." He placed the book on the table in front of her. "It's all about the Yankees."

Rachel pulled the book out of the bag graciously and said in a musical tone, "Why, thank you, Squid."

Squid became more animated. "It has lots of pictures and the history of the Yankees. It has a lot of neat statistics too." Rachel opened the book and Squid pushed himself to speak. "Did you know that only three Yankees had back-to-back seasons with forty home runs or more? You'd think it would be Reggie Jackson or Roger Maris, but it isn't. I'm hoping it will be Don Mattingly one day, but he isn't one of them yet. Although I think he is the greatest first baseman of all time. Of course Babe Ruth is one of them and also Mickey Mantle. But guess who the other one is?"

Rachel thumbed through the colored photos. "This is so nice . . ."

"It's Lou Gehrig." Squid surged ahead. "It's all in the book there. Someday I want to go to a Yankees game when I work up the nerve. I want to—"

"Oh, Jason!" Rachel turned around quickly and grabbed a young man's arm. "Come here, I want you to meet some people." Rachel still held the Yankees book in one hand. She closed it and put it on top of the plastic bag beside her. Jason was blond and tan with high cheekbones. He had a bowl of oatmeal and a spoon in his hand.

"Just taking a break from my that's-no-ladle-that's-my-knife routine on the serving line." He grinned at Rachel as he sat down. Rachel exploded in laughter and Jason continued to grin. Obviously it was some previous joke they had been sharing.

"These are the three musketeers." Rachel gestured to the men seated near her. Her eyes sparkled in a new way. "Bonehead, Squid, and Unc."

Bonehead reached across the table and shook Jason's hand. Bonehead had some oatmeal on his palm and he passed it on to Jason's hand. Jason discreetly wiped his hand on a paper napkin. "Nice to meet you, Bonehead."

Squid just nodded at Jason. He hated Jason immediately. He touched the bat next to his leg quietly.

Unc reached out with both hands across the table and shook Jason's hand vigorously. "Welcome, welcome, my friend. So you are the new volunteer. I want to hear about how you came to be here and what you think of things here.

I'm a born-again Christian too, and I want to hear about your spiritual journey.

Jason threw up his hands and laughed good-naturedly. "I'd love to talk and the things you have asked are the most important to me. But give me a moment to catch my breath!" He turned to Rachel and started hyperventilating and then let his tongue hang out. She giggled. "I've got silverware on the mind here, and I need to get my bearings. First of all, why are you called Unc?"

"Because I am so avuncular. Most of the people I hang around with, like Squid here, are much younger than I am. I am like their uncle. It's my role in the neighborhood. We all have a role, a destiny, don't you think? Squid is called Squid because he is known to get squid at the Chinese takeout at the corner if he ever has the money. I do not know what his real name is. He's never told me. Bonehead's name, I suppose, is self-explanatory."

Bonehead gave a grunt that may have been disapproval, and he shoved Unc.

"Nicknames are very important here in this neighborhood." Unc was getting expansive. "Some people have nicknames because they are on the run from the law. Others have run away from their family and don't want to be found. For others, well, it is just kind of fun, or maybe they want to start over, to be 'born again,' so to speak." Unc eyed Jason to see how he was taking things so far. "Others want to leave an impression that may help them. For example, there is a colorful gentleman in this area right now named Saw. Saw got his name here because when he was in jail, he had nothing better to do but file the two canine teeth beside his front teeth into points."

Unc bared his own teeth and motioned to the upper teeth next to the four front teeth. "Don't ask me what dental challenges such a move presents. When he grins, and he does have an intimidating grin, one could get the impression of a saw, if you know what I mean. I wouldn't be surprised if he gave himself that name. It would go with his persona."

"You know, that is so amazing," Rachel said. She had that earnest tone in her voice now. Squid knew she was going to say something about God. This humorless earnestness was one reason some people didn't like Rachel. No more joking now. Squid didn't mind. "You know, the name of someone is so important in the Bible. In the Bible, the name represents a person's nature or character. When Jesus gives Simon a new name, it means something important. In the end of the Bible, Jesus promises he will give us a new name, which nobody knows."

By this time, Rachel had lost both Bonehead and Unc, so she looked Squid right in the eye. Squid nodded in encouragement, although what she was saying was vaguely unsettling to him. Rachel continued. "That's why the Lord's Prayer is so important. That's why Jesus says, 'Hallowed be thy *name*' right at the first. God's name, or character, is important, and he takes our name, or character, seriously. Very seriously. You know at the mission service when we pray in Jesus' name?"

Larry, with the sagging sombrero, was sitting at another

table. While Rachel spoke, he had taken his soiled sports shirt off. He had a T-shirt on underneath it. Then he took his bowl in one hand and his shirt in the other and moved to Rachel's table. As Rachel continued to speak so earnestly to Squid, he sat down close to her and put his shirt over the Yankees book that lay between them. "Hi, Rachel," he said and grinned.

Rachel looked at his hat-for-the-day. "Hi, you gringo," she said and laughed.

Unc saw his chance to change the direction of the conversation. Turning back to Jason, he said, "So in light of the significance of names in my world and your world, why are you here? Are you looking for adventure, or as our modern-day Jason, are you seeking a golden fleece?"

"Just rope me to the mast so I won't be torn by so much beauty. Or was that Odysseus?" Jason turned to Rachel and made his eyes bug out. She laughed again. "No, Unc, I guess I am here because I want to learn what service is." Now it was Jason's time to sound earnest. Squid rolled his eyes and sighed audibly. "Yes, God has been working in my life the last few years. I guess you'd say I grew up in a privileged background, and I am not used to the surroundings here. They stun me. I can't believe that we are twenty blocks, *twenty blocks* away from Wall Street, one of the richest places in the world, and here kids can't read and adults are having to scrounge and stand in line for some oatmeal."

"So you feel that you can be of some help to change that." Unc was being his most avuncular. He leaned back and put the fingers of both hands together.

"Well . . . yes." Jason was taking Unc very seriously. Squid began to shift around in his seat nervously.

"And you think that your work here is part of your commitment to Christ." Unc continued in reassuring tones.

Jason paused to think before he responded. "Yes, I do. Look, I know I don't know much yet, but being here really makes me think that things are insane. I mean, look at all the wealth in this city and look at all the unhappiness in this room. Think of the Christians sitting in air-conditioned sanctuaries and plush seats while we work with this." Jason picked up his oatmeal bowl. Squid wished he could talk like that. Rachel had folded her hands and was listening intently.

Jason continued. "I guess that's why I'm here. Christ changed my life, but at college you talk and talk and talk. What I like about this," again he lifted up the bowl, "is that it is not theoretical—it is very concrete, tangible."

"That oatmeal sure is concrete," Squid ventured. Rachel didn't laugh.

"So you think it is good that this mission is here," Unc continued.

"Yes," Jason said without hesitating.

"And you think it is good that Squid here gets a check for mental disability." Squid's face turned the color of a tomato. He had been hiding his hands, but now he began to bite his thumb furiously.

"If it is necessary, absolutely." Everyone at the table was looking at Unc.

"Do you think it is good that Squid and I can sleep

until noon if we want and that Squid gives some of his money to me?"

"I don't know." Jason looked confused but not intimidated.

"Do you think that other hardworking people should start work at six in the morning so that we can have that chance to sleep through the morning? Do you think it is good that kindhearted churches like this one give food to people like me so that I can read all day and have money for drinks?" Unc's voice got louder and he wasn't waiting for a response. "Did you know that because there are several mission-type churches here in this neighborhood, people come from all over because they can stay in an abandoned building for free, get free meals with people like you serving them, then spend taxpayer's money for crack?" Unc's tone was getting more belligerent.

"Do you know what a *squat* is, Jason? It's a city-owned building that people have illegally occupied. Did you know that Squid and I live in a squat? Rachel is right. Names are important. How would you like to have your domicile, your place of residence, referred to as a squat? You see, here in this area, the word *squat* is more important as a noun than a verb. We live in a squat. We don't know squat. We don't have squat. We don't *do* squat. We don't give a squat. People say we're not worth squat. Did you ever think about that—when you took your nice shower this morning and Squid here used a bucket for a toilet—did you ever think what your nice little work is creating in this neighborhood?"

The silence made Squid feel that a fight was about to break out. People from other tables had gotten quiet and were listening to Unc. At this point, Larry got up. "Gotta go," he said. With both hands he picked up the shirt and something hard and flat underneath it. Squid gave Larry a nod but looked right back at Unc and Jason.

Jason was not flustered. "I thought you said you were a born-again Christian."

"I'm a very backslidden born-again Christian, Jason. I'm also a backslidden Buddhist. I've also been to enough missions to know a lot of gospel songs from a lot of old donated hymnbooks. Isaac Watts is my favorite songwriter. I know that if I use the right words, I may get more from a church. How long do you plan to be here, Jason?"

For the first time, Jason dropped his eyes momentarily from Unc's. "For the rest of the summer."

"Oh, so you are going to stay here for the summer and help people like me survive so I can continue to do some recreational drinking and drugs, and then you will go back to your life and tell stories about your 'meaningful' summer? Will it help your résumé for graduate school? Will you take a picture of me in my blanket and Bonehead with his mop handle? You know, I don't mind, but Bonehead and Squid here don't like to be treated like a *project*." Another silence. Squid couldn't tell if the bitterness in Unc's voice was faked for effect or if it was real.

Jason did not wait long to respond. "I don't know what I am going to do after this summer, and there is some truth to your accusations. But I don't agree with your generalization about places like this. There need to be places where there are no questions asked and people who simply need a helping hand can get some help. Sure, some people will take advantage of this kind of giving, but the alternative I suppose you are suggesting is one where we are hardhearted to all people, some of whom simply need a meal, maybe even just a little oatmeal, or maybe someone to simply know their *name*, to get them through the day."

"Yes, but you will get more attention if you say the right Christian words, believe me," Unc said in a stronger tone. "And can use the words of Isaac Watts."

"That may be true, but you have to start somewhere. I don't see anyone crowding around the poetry cafe on the next block asking for help or getting a meal from the storefront psychics in this area. At least the mission is doing something, even if it is sometimes misguided. Who knows, it might even touch some backslidden Christian Buddhist."

"Yes, you are right. Your kindness might just fund a backslidden Christian Buddhist so that he can drink himself to death. That is a very helpful attitude, and I thank you." Unc laughed and nodded to Rachel. "You got a good one this time, Rachel," Unc said as he motioned his head toward Jason. "He doesn't mind dishing a little out. Let's see how he does here in the neighborhood." Unc looked at Jason with less-than-kind eyes. Jason stared back. An awkward pause settled on the table.

"My disability checks are only temporary," Squid said quietly.

Unc laughed again and said, "My apologies for including you in my discussion, Squid. For me, you are more sane than those dispensing the checks, but I will stop speaking." Unc held his hands up and motioned toward Jason. "Don't get me started!"

Squid turned to Rachel. "Anyway, Rachel, do you still want to see the circus animals come through the midtown tunnel? They do it at 4:30 in the morning when there's not much traffic. They'll be walking the elephants through on foot. I don't know why they have to do it that way."

"Sure. Maybe the elephants have to open their *trunks* for the inspectors." Rachel had lost her earnest look and was all smiles again. "What time do I need to meet you?"

"At 4:00 a.m. in front of the parking lot close to the bus stop." Squid spoke in his most authoritative voice. He had practiced that phrase over and over this morning before dawn as he waited for Saw.

"Great. Can Jason come too if he wants?"

A storm crossed Squid's face. He forgot about hiding his chewed-up thumbs and squeezed the top of the table until his thumbs turned white. "Sure," he said in a dead tone. He was working hard to keep himself from turning the table over in anger. His eyes rested on the empty space next to Rachel's seat.

"Where's the Yankees book?" he asked.

Rachel turned and took in a deep breath. "It was here just a minute ago." She looked under the table and on the chairs with an earnest expression. "It's gone. Oh, nooo."

She looked again under the table. "I am so sorry, Squid. I don't know what happened."

Squid couldn't even nod.

Unc stood up and said, "I've got to keep this warrior here moving." He motioned to Squid, who looked very pale as he stood up. "I'm the Virgil to Squid's Dante today. I need to walk him through the inferno." This time even Jason had no clue what Unc was talking about. Jason and Rachel stood, and Unc came around the table to shake Jason's hand one more time.

Jason reached out his hand with his fingers frozen in a mock claw. "Sorry, I would shake your hand but I have silverware server's cramp." Rachel burst out laughing again at another inside joke with Jason.

As Rachel and Unc crowded around Jason, Squid quickly took the gum out from between his cheek and his teeth, reached over the table, and shoved it with his thumb deep into Jason's oatmeal. When he pulled out his hand back from the bowl, there was only a little dimple where his thumb had been. No one had seen him.

Squid wrapped his hands in his T-shirt, nodded his head to Rachel, and struggled to rasp out "See ya," before he walked out the door. It was all he could do.

CHAPTER 5

SQUID PACED BACK and forth on the sidewalk outside, waiting for Unc and Bonehead to finish chatting with Jason and Rachel. "Come on, come on," he said with clenched teeth. Squid cursed Larry. He felt for his bat beneath his pant leg and looked up and down the street.

Unc laughed expansively as he walked out the door, but was aware enough of Squid's turmoil to be respectfully silent when he caught up with Squid, who was walking quickly away from the mission building with determined steps. As Bonehead toddled along behind and finally caught up with the two, Squid turned to Bonehead and snatched the plastic mop handle out of his hands and slammed it over and over again on a fire hydrant. Squid roared as the mop splintered and shredded. Part of it flew in the air in a graceful arc and landed on a car nearby. Nobody on the street even looked up. They didn't care.

Unc continued to walk and stretched his hand out from his sheet to put his arm around Bonehead. He moved respectfully, giving Squid some time to calm down. Quietly he said to Bonehead, "Sometimes the scariest people are the most scared. Everything will be all right in a few minutes."

All three of them continued to head toward the park in silence. When they got to the corner, Squid lifted his eyes. In front of him were a hundred makeshift dwellings scattered around the park behind benches or iron fences. They were made out of cardboard and blankets and a few haphazard boards nailed together. A few structures were old camping tents, which had found their way, probably through churches, to this humid, dirty place. In the hot sun the park smelled like urine and old trash. All the grass in the park was gone. The ground around the trees had been stomped down by many feet until it was as hard as the sidewalk. The structures had cropped up day by day since Squid had been there. He never even noticed them, but after his breakfast, he felt as though he was looking at the park through Jason's eyes. Squid wondered what he would have thought as a child if someone then had told him that he would ever live in a place like this.

The three slowed down as they entered the shade of the park trees and the warm, living ambience of the home-less tribal village. "We may need to stop and strategize a moment," Unc said. "You don't know who you might run into here. Saw should be sleeping by now."

Again Squid touched the bat underneath his pant leg. He didn't think about things the way Unc did. The three slowed their walk down so much that they were hardly moving. Squid felt like everyone was watching him. A familiar face came up to them.

"I thought you were going to go to sleep, Ratchet," Unc said.

Ratchet was still holding his snake on his arm but was no longer smiling. "Snappy needed to see some of her friends in the park." He spoke slowly, motioning toward his python. Then he looked directly at Squid. "Why you trying to mess with Saw, man? He was just here in the park saying how you ripped him off and now he's going to take care of you. That guy can give you the creeps. He's always talking black magic and that Santeria garbage and about sacrificing animals for power. I don't think he does it, man, but he's always talking about it, like he's trying to prove something. You remember Duckie who used to live here in the park, but nobody's seen him for a long time? Saw said today he took care of him. Cut him up and put him in three garbage bags with bricks and threw him in the river. He just says things like that in the park to try to freak people out, I guess. But you know, Squid, he does keep his word, and when he says something, it happens."

"I didn't rip him off," Squid said feebly.

"What time did he leave?" Unc asked.

"Like ten or fifteen minutes ago." Ratchet turned to look directly at Squid again. "I don't think you should be hanging out in the park right now, man. Saw doesn't really have friends here, but everybody is pretty charged up about what he said about you. That was low to take his money. What were you thinking?"

A person Squid did not know got up and started walking toward them. He had a hammer in his hand. Other people stood outside their tents and just stared at Squid. It was too hot for them to say anything. They looked like zombies. "We were just getting ready to leave," Unc said. "Thanks for the orientation, Ratchet." Unc put his hand to Squid's back and turned him around. All three started walking in the direction they had come.

They moved quickly away from the park. Squid felt as though everyone was staring at his back. They turned the first corner they reached and slowed down a little when they were out of sight. Unc took charge. They walked in a zigzag direction, backtracking from the park, until they were a number of blocks away on a side street. They walked to the middle of the block. Squid knew where they were going. It was a spot Unc liked to frequent by himself, a small "vest pocket park." When abandoned buildings were torn down in the area, small city-owned lots emerged as a part of the landscape. As time went on, the city didn't seem to mind as people planted trees and bushes in them. Blocks put in their own chain-link fences for protection and hence provided another place for people to hang out.

This particular little park was often abandoned and sometimes the lock was unlocked. The lock was open today and no one was there. It was a good decision for now. No one would look for Squid there. Unc walked right in and sat down on a milk crate with a grunt. Somewhere Bonehead had found another four-foot-long stick—this time, a sturdy tree limb—and was now looking around for some pebbles to hit like baseballs.

It was getting very muggy, and Squid sat down on the ground under a bush. Suddenly, he felt very tired.

"Let's think about your battle plan, grandson. You have successfully maneuvered through breakfast, but apparently the chase is still on."

"Oh, Unc, this is the worst day of my life. Breakfast was a nightmare."

Unc was close enough to gently pat Squid on the head. He pulled out the bottle from his front pocket. "Yes, I imagine it was pretty difficult. It is hard to watch a gift you're risking your life for snatched away as if it were as disposable as a paper plate. Pearls snatched away by swine and all that."

"Larry did it and I saw it all and I didn't even realize what he was doing. I am going to kill him and roast him like a hot dog."

"Well, it is hard to be too hard on Larry. From one perspective, you know, Larry did to you what you did to Saw." Unc adjusted the sheet that was draped around him. "Is Larry a friend of Saw's? Sometimes petty people make petty alliances."

Squid refused to listen. "I'm going to kill Saw too for calling me a cheater in front of everybody." Squid said this with much less conviction.

"Well, since you're not planning to kill him right now, I think your best plan is to wait here and let things cool down." Unc adjusted the milk crate so that he could lean back against the fence. He cradled the bottle in his hand as if it contained holy water. "You see, grandson, the day has changed already from what you thought. There is only a certain amount of value in planning ahead, you know." Unc took a slow and delicate sip. "You can't really choreograph things too much. Life is more like a boxing match than a ballet. You've got to be more like Ali than Baryshnikov."

"What are you saying, Unc? Are you saying that I ought to hit Larry?"

Unc smiled and motioned his hand mysteriously in the air, as if he were a war chief at a council. "No, no, no. I'm saying that you have to be prepared, but you're going to have to be prepared to improvise. At the split second. You see, life is more like jazz than a symphony. You don't get a score of every note. Sometimes you're just given a theme. Sometimes your life is a variation on a theme that is already there, and you are put here, in this moment of time, to develop it. But you can't play anything exactly the way it happened before. You've got to develop it in the moment. So you've really got to be more like Miles Davis than Leonard Bernstein."

"Are those guys boxers too? I've never heard of them."

"No, no, no, grandson." Unc stroked his moustache. "Although boxing was a hobby for Miles." Unc took a sip. "What an interesting connection, Squid. I think I will proclaim Miles, fighter-improviser, as your patron saint for the day." Unc lifted his bottle in salute. "Anyway, my point is that you ought to stay here and rest for awhile because you really don't know what is going to happen next."

"I guess you're right," Squid said as he straightened out

his leg so that his bat would not pinch him. The day seemed to stretch out before him forever. How was he ever going to make it to four o'clock in the morning when he would see Rachel again? As he sat on the ground, with the day getting hotter, he tried to resist the boredom coming on him. Squid got up and walked over to the other side of the lot so that he could see the clock in the Con Ed tower. It said eleven o'clock. Funny how a sense of danger can last only so long. He had nothing to do. No radio so that he could listen to a baseball game or some sports recap. Unc hated baseball anyway and wouldn't talk to Squid about it. Bonehead was throwing rocks into the air and hitting them with his new stick. Squid went back over and sat by Unc.

"Unc, do you ever just think how strange it is, just being alive? I mean, like, here we are, and blood is flowing through my brain, and this world is going around this sun, and I don't really know where I came from or what I'm doing here. Maybe I'll die today and you'll remember me for a little while but you'll keep going and then someday die of liver damage or something and Bonehead here doesn't hardly remember my name now. If I die today, I will end up in the morgue on First Avenue and what's left of my mom, wherever she is, will never know what happened to me. There won't even be a funeral. That's my life. That's it. I mean, it sometimes all seems so *strange,* and if I think about it, it makes my stomach feel like I'm going down an elevator too fast."

Unc took a drink. "Actually, I try not to think about that, Squid. That's why I like to read. It keeps me from thinking about things like that. Reading is a wonderful drug for me to guard against life."

"Unc, you know that poem on your wall about the three angels? This is going to sound funny. Do you, like, do you really *believe* that? I mean, that there really are three angels that want to do good for us, that they really are here and all?"

Unc blew air out of his mouth in derision. "Of course not."

"So why do you take the time to write that stuff out and put it on the wall? You don't even believe it."

"Because it's so beautiful. It was written by a great, great poet. It's not true in the way you're thinking it's true, but it is true in another way." Unc put his bottle back in his pocket. "It's so beautiful that I guess it makes me wish it were true, even though I know it's not."

"Then you're not a backslidden born-again Christian or Buddhist or anything, are you?"

"Nah," Unc said. "I just say things like that to break the monotony, I guess. Monotony is the great battleground for people that live like you and me, Squid. We're not rushing anywhere to do anything. Monotony is our profession, but you can't place your faith even in monotony. One day, all of a sudden, in a desert of boredom, your life takes on a storybook character, at least for a moment." Unc shifted his legs around on the ground. "Someday I've got to tell you all about Miles Davis. Then you'll understand a lot more about what I am talking about here."

Squid picked up a piece of red crayon that was lying in the dust. Thinking hard, he peeled the paper off the crayon. "Do you ever wish you could just do one thing, Unc, one thing so well it was like hitting a home run? One thing that would be like hitting the ball out of the park in the World Series with the crowd going wild. Just one time, I think everybody ought to have that feeling."

"Life is funny that way, grandson. Just when the probabilities tell you for sure that nothing good is going to happen, something surprises you. Those little slips in the monotony are what keep me going."

Squid started peeling red off the side of the crayon with his fingernail. "I mean, like, what if, Unc? What if some great Yankee player, like Don Mattingly, for instance, became my friend because he liked my looks when I got his autograph. And what if, just on a joke, he worked it so I could suit up in some game? And what if when I was suited up, they interviewed me on the radio and everyone knew about it. And what if we were way ahead and someone egged Don on and the crowd was calling my name and the manager said I could go in to bat, just on a fluke. And what if, on that first pitch, Unc, I swung with all my might, and even though I couldn't even see the ball coming at me at a hundred miles an hour, it happened to come right where my bat was swinging. And what if, by chance, the ball hit my bat right at that sweet spot, just by chance. Think of the roar of the crowd at the crack of that bat. Think of them all standing up and watching it fly over the fence. What do you think that would feel like to start trotting around the bases with everybody shouting and rooting for you because no one expected you to even make contact at all, and if you did make contact, it would just be a foul ball? The crowd would go crazy. That would be something to stamp your foot down on home plate and have all the Yankees running out to slap you on the back. Wouldn't that be great, Unc?"

"It'd be like winning the lottery, grandson. It's improbability piled upon improbability, but it's got to happen sometime to somebody. It's like that one monkey who typed long enough until by chance he typed out a play by Shakespeare. It would have to happen if he typed long enough. That's what stories are all about, the shocking improbabilities that punctuate our inevitable, endless monotony." Unc gestured here across the expanse of abandoned buildings he could see across the street.

"But look at Bonehead, Unc. You know, something like that could really happen to him, if he weren't so retarded and people could understand what he said. Do you know how hard it is to hit a little piece of gravel with a stick that size and make it go where you want it to go? And he hits it almost every time. It's his only talent. Bonehead could play for the Yankees, if he weren't such a bonehead." A rock whizzed by Squid's face. "Hey! Don't hit those things this way, you moron!"

Bonehead turned the other way and tossed up another rock. As it came down, his stick whistled through the air and hit the rock with a crack. The rock flew out of the little park and hit the building across the street.

"Wow! Another home run. Outta the park! Bonehead Mantle, with back-to-back seasons with forty home runs each!" Squid got up and took the stick out of Bonehead's hands. "Let me try that." Squid threw up a piece of rock and took a swing. Missed it. He did it again. Another miss. Again and again he tried but nicked the rock only once. "How does Bonehead do that?" he said.

"Whatjathink, whatjathink?" Bonehead said from another corner of the park. He came to Squid with his hands cupped to protect something. Very gently he showed Squid what he was protecting. A tiny baby squirrel was shivering in his palm. Squid went back to the tree where Bonehead came from and looked up. He couldn't see anything.

"It must have fallen from the tree. Man, it's so tiny. Look, he's shaking even though it is so hot."

Bonehead wouldn't let Squid get too close. He nudged Squid away with his elbow and sat down.

"Look, Bonehead, he looks naked. He doesn't have hardly any hair. Look how scared he is. He's still shivering, man. Let me hold him."

Bonehead hunched his shoulders up and let his whole body be a protection for the squirrel.

"Come on, Bonehead, let me look. Man, this little squirrel needs help. I'd hit you with my bat if you weren't holding that thing. Why don't you put the little thing back under the tree, man. Maybe the mom will come back and take care of it."

Bonehead shook his head. He started rocking back and forth, shielding his little treasure from Squid.

"Yeah, maybe you're right. The mama might not know what to do with it now. Will a squirrel take back its baby once humans have messed with it? Or maybe the mom is dead and can't take care of it anymore." Squid hovered over Bonehead and tried to get a better look. "Man, he looks so helpless. We can't let him go for a minute, Bonehead. A rat will eat him or something." The baby squirrel curled up in Bonehead's hand. It looked like it was going to sleep.

"I wonder what you feed a squirrel that age," Squid said. He walked over to ask Unc, but Unc was sound asleep, still propped up on the crate, wrapped in his dirty sheet. "I wonder if I bought him some milk, he would drink it." Squid walked through the gate to look down the street to see if a corner store was on that block. He saw one. As he looked the other way down the block, he saw a solitary man walking away from the park. He was almost to the corner. He was wearing a familiar sombrero.

———

Quickly Squid put his hand on the bat inside his pants and ran three steps toward the sombrero. Then he stopped, every muscle tense. He felt like a car at a stoplight when the brake and the gas are floored at the same time. He wanted to surge forward but something held him back. He felt sick to his stomach.

"Unc, wake up. I think we need to get outta here. I just saw Larry, and, I don't know how to say it, but I think I gotta leave. Like really quick. Like right now."

Unc rubbed his eyes and said, "OK." Unc rubbed his knees and checked to make sure his book and his bottle were there.

Unc was moving way too slow for Squid. "Look, you bring Bonehead and meet me at the corner store in a minute." The corner store was in the opposite direction from where Larry was headed. Squid couldn't contain himself any longer. He ran.

It only took Unc and Bonehead a few minutes to get to the store, but it seemed like forever to Squid. Squid watched the windows from inside the store. He didn't know the young man with a moustache behind the counter. The salsa music from the radio playing seemed so happy; the air conditioning seemed so cool. The man behind the counter stared at Squid. It was a little threatening. Squid made a big show of digging into his pocket and pulling out enough money for a small carton of milk.

"What do baby squirrels eat?" Squid asked the cashier with a moustache as he bought the milk. The man didn't say a word but just stared at Squid. "Do you speak English? Aw, forget it." Squid looked out the window again, terrified that he might see a sombrero. Finally, when he could think of no other reason to stand at the counter with the staring man, he gingerly stepped outside. At that moment, Unc and Bonehead walked up to the door. Bonehead was still cradling the baby squirrel in one hand and held his new stick in his other.

"My apologies for being delayed, Squid. Bonehead and I had a little discussion about this accursed squirrel."

"Did you see Larry or . . . anyone else?"

"No, Squid, but I am a firm believer in trusting your gut. Who knows what your animal instincts are telling you?

Or whatever it is that makes you do the crazy things you do. I vote that we move to another block right now."

Unc took charge again, moving to get as far away from the vest pocket park as quickly as possible.

After awhile, they slowed their pace. Squid remembered his carton of milk. "Let me have a look at the squirrel, Bonehead. Aww, look, man. It's shivering again, and it must be a hundred degrees today." Bonehead and Squid stopped at the corner and squatted down. "Maybe the little thing is hungry. Look, Bonehead, let me put a drop of milk on your finger and see if it will take some." Bonehead held his brown, crusty forefinger out and Squid poured some milk on it. Bonehead tenderly held his finger close to the little squirrel's mouth. "Look, Bonehead, it's trying it. Maybe it's not an *it*, maybe it's a she. Do you know how to tell if a squirrel is a he or a she? I don't want to scare it . . . her by checking. Look, she's drinking a little more." Squid rubbed his hands together in excitement. "Look how shy she is. We ought to give her a name, Bonehead. What do you think we could call her? What about Flicker? She's as small as a flicker of light. No, she's like a flicker of hope. She could go out any minute. Look at Flicker. She's drinking like crazy now."

Unc sighed loudly as he stood beside the two eager parents hovering over Flicker. "Gentlemen, pardon my interruption, but I will have to find a place to sit down and rest these battered appendages of mine. How long do you plan to take with your new ward? It may be time to return it to nature and let nature take her course with it."

"Just a minute, Unc." Squid turned to Bonehead, who was still patiently giving the squirrel little drops of milk. "We need to make a home for this little thing. Look, I've got some new socks back at the squat. I've never worn them. The mission gave them to me. Flicker needs a place she can stay safe in. A place that's clean, like a nest or something. Let's go back to our place and see if we can't work something out for her."

Unc stroked his hair, which was still courageously attempting to defy gravity. "I don't know about going back to the squat, Squid."

"What do you mean? Look, Saw needs to be scared of *me*, not the other way around. Besides, we have to take care of this little baby squirrel. And anyway, doesn't your Chinese ninja guy say that we need to do the unexpected. Saw has told everyone he's looking for me. He won't expect me to be at *home*. And you guys can go ahead of me and give me the signal that everything is OK. You can make Bonehead go first."

The three turned toward the squat. The street was drearily humid. The trash along the sidewalk smelled more like rotten vegetables and urine as the heat rose. Everything seemed to be moving in slow motion. "Lookitdat," Bonehead said. He had slipped the baby squirrel in his front shirt pocket. The squirrel snuggled down and looked as though it felt safer there.

"No, Bonehead, put her in your other pocket. It doesn't have a button so it won't be hurting his head. Squid reached in Bonehead's other pocket and pulled a scrap of paper out.

It was a Social Security printout. Squid read the top line. "Angel Jose Martinez. This isn't yours, Bonehead. You're not Puerto Rican."

"Yep, yep," Bonehead said.

"Well your skin is dark enough, but you don't speak Spanish, do you?"

"Nope, nope."

"Stop carrying other people's stuff around, Bonehead." Squid threw the paper on the ground. Bonehead held the baby squirrel in his pocket with one hand and scooped up the piece of paper with the other, shoving it in his pants. Then, with gentle caution, he moved Flicker from the pocket with the button to the pocket without one. When the three got to the block where their squat was located, Squid stayed leaning against a chain-link fence around the corner. He looked up and down the avenues and chewed on his thumb. Bonehead and Unc walked down the street and entered the squat. "At least the door is open," Squid said to himself.

Unc emerged and gave a thumbs-up sign. Squid took big strides down the street with purpose, favoring his left leg. The ladies that were looking out the windows this morning were still there. Now Squid looked at them differently. They seemed like spies. It seemed to Squid as though they were looking at him with a particularly disapproving scowl. Squid scowled back. He ducked in the front door. The hallway was much cooler and damper than the street outside. "Almost like air-conditioning," Squid said.

Unc and Bonehead had waited for him. Squid tried to

figure out why he was feeling so upset again. Why had he suggested that all three of them come back to the squat? What was Squid thinking? That must be it. This was the second time Bonehead had been in his squat in one day. He didn't know what was going on inside of himself, he just knew he didn't like it.

A few people were stirring on the second floor now, which was smelling worse as the day got hotter. Most of the people were still motionless on dirty mattresses. One young man, called Chaos, was sitting up on his mattress and rubbing his eyes. He had olive skin and long Rastafarian dreadlocks. Little pieces of paper and twigs were stuck in his hair all the way down his back. "Hey, Squid," he said in a monotone. Chaos was the closest thing to a leader that the second-floor group had. "Molly came looking for you and says you owe her money fast."

"Molly came by here? To the second floor? Today? How did she get in? What did she want?"

"I don't know. She just said that you cheated them and that she and Saw were going to make you pay. Why are you hanging with those guys, man? They're like bad karma. Saw is a walking powder keg. He's a buzz saw."

"How long ago did she come?" Unc asked.

Chaos kept rubbing his eyes. "I don't know, man. She woke me up."

"Did she leave or did she go upstairs."

"She left, man," Chaos said, a little offended. "We've got rules here. I'm not going to let her go upstairs." He moved to lie down again to let them know the conversation was over.

"Yeah, right," Squid skeptically replied. He turned to Unc. "I can't believe Molly was right here in the squat. The nerve. What was she thinking?" The three began climbing the stairs to the third floor, Squid moving very slowly. "I feel sorry for that woman, and I hate her for staying with Saw. Her nose looks like it has been broken twenty times. She looks so old and pathetic. But she will do anything Saw tells her to do. She follows him around like a whipped dog. He must beat her like a dog too. I bet he cuts her up where people can't see what he's done. Bonehead, you go in first and see if Molly is there."

Bonehead had one hand covering his pocket to protect his little furry ward, the other holding his bat. He marched upstairs, and after a moment, Unc and Squid followed him. Other than the noise of traffic from the streets below, the floor was extremely quiet. You could hear one horsefly buzzing around the toilet bucket, but that was it.

Squid went to his corner of the room and sorted through his soiled but folded clothes. "Here's some brand new socks that I got at the clothing closet. Flicker can have them." Squid picked up a shoebox he had found on the street. "And here is a little box that could be her home if she needs one. Everybody needs some place where they feel they have protection. Here, this can be her squat, a place that she always knows is here. This 'home' used to belong to some shoes. Now it belongs to a squirrel."

Squid arranged the box the best he could. He took an old fork and made a hole in the top of the lid of the box. He helped Bonehead take the little baby out of his pocket and placed it gently in the box. Squid got the bottle of milk and edged Bonehead away from the box. "Let me feed Flicker this time, you moron." Squid dipped his finger in the carton of milk and put the finger with a drop of milk next to the squirrel's mouth. The little squirrel began to lick his finger. "Look at this, Bonehead. Flicker is still hungry. Aww, look at her. She's not shivering anymore. Look, she feels safe."

Squid and Bonehead kept nudging each other away from the best view of the box. Finally, Squid placed the lid gently on the box. "Let's let her rest for awhile, what do you say, Bonehead?"

Squid left Bonehead sitting next to the shoe box and staring at the closed lid. "You stay here and guard her, Bonehead. Now, I'm leaving you in charge. Don't let anything happen to her." Squid walked over to sit down with Unc, who had swathed himself with two extra sheets. The hair that had been standing up on the top of his head was drooping in the heat. Now only a portion of his hair stood up in a shallow loop, like the top of Woody Woodpecker's head.

Unc was reading a different book taken from his pile. It had the word *Gilgamesh* in the title. Squid had never heard of it. Squid let out a big sigh and wrapped both hands in his shirt. "Unc, this has been the worst day of my life." Squid stretched his legs out on the ground covered with blankets and paperbacks. "What do I do now? Saw not only has his slaves, like Molly, looking for me, but he's told everybody and probably has other punks out to get me."

Unc kept reading and didn't even look up. Finally, he closed the book with firmness and looked at Squid. "It's time to split up. We can't stay here. Things are starting to feel more dangerous. You go down the fire escape and I will take Bonehead out the front. Someone may be watching." Unc picked up two more paperback books. "I'm not going to my normal place. I'm going to Tenth and C and I'm going to sit in the shade and read. Do you have any money to help with my liquification?"

"Stop pacing around the room, Bonehead! There's no more rats up here." Squid could feel the irritation rise. He started tugging at his bat when Bonehead steered close to the wall where Squid had hidden his envelope behind a brick. Squid reached in his pocket and pulled out two crumpled dollar bills. "Here, Unc, take these. Are you sure it is best for me to be alone now?"

"Look at us. A drunk, an idiot, and a nut job. We are begging to be hunted down. When detectives in the movie chased the Hole in the Wall Gang, they always split up, didn't they?" Unc pulled out an index card and began writing. "Remember, think like a warrior. Do the unexpected. When you get to the point where you really have no idea what to do next, read this card." Unc handed Squid the card.

"Bonehead, stop roaming around!" Squid shouted in a fury. "OK, Unc, but I'm really scared. I don't want to be forgotten. I don't want to disappear like Duckie. I don't want to be just a story that you remember and tell some other young kid in a few years."

Bonehead had found a rat hole. He was on his hands and knees, poking the opening with his stick. He crawled closer and closer to the brick that hid the envelope. Squid stood up and looked around with a shiver. Then he looked back at Bonehead, stomped toward him, and gave him a savage kick to the rear. Bonehead's whole body went forward and he hit his head on the wall. Unc let out a chuckle.

But it was Squid who screamed. "Ooooouch! Oh, my toe! You idiot, you broke my toe!" Squid sat on the ground and began to take his tennis shoe off. When he got the sock off, the joint of his big toe was red and swelling. Bonehead just sat on the floor and rubbed his head.

Unc laughed. "Ah, Squid, you're just like Paul of Tarsus. The harder you kick, the more it hurts you. Is that a metaphor for your life or what?"

On the floor below, the voice of Chaos and some other visitor wafted up the stairway. Squid could hear that Chaos had his businesslike voice on. The visitor must be someone he didn't know very well.

"Hurry up and get your shoe on, grandson, and go down the fire escape. Bonehead and I will face the visitor, whoever he or she might be and whatever tidings they bring, for good or for ill. I'll tell them you went to Coney Island. Bonehead, you bring your bat and come over and stand in front of me. You will be the first line of defense for whoever this merciless marauder might be. I'm going to conceal myself in the closet and be the second line of defense."

"I'm not leaving until Bonehead leaves. I don't like him roaming around here," Squid hissed as he quickly put his shoe on.

"OK, OK, I will escort him to the door right now." Unc got up and approached the stunned Bonehead and gently nudged Bonehead's elbow. Bonehead was still rubbing his head but got up and began to drift to the door. He picked up the squirrel and put her in one pocket and took a new sock to put in the other pocket. "Take Flicker's home with you, Bonehead," Squid said. "Everybody needs a home."

Bonehead nodded his head resolutely and placed his hand around the pocket with Flicker in it.

"You better take good care of her!" Squid limped to the window. "I am going to kill Bonehead. Why couldn't this have happened on another day?"

Unc gave Squid the thumbs-up. "Into the mouth of the wolf!"

"Yeah, right," Squid said as he climbed out the window.

CHAPTER 6

SQUID WAS NOT exactly a big fan of heights. But there he was, standing on the rusty fire escape, clutching the iron handle for dear life. The iron on the railings and steps was very thin in places. The building itself had been abandoned for a long time, at least since the seventies, and the fire escape probably hadn't been serviced for decades before that. Blackened windows showed that fires had charred the building more than once.

I probably shouldn't climb down this, he thought. Yet, as Squid stood on the flimsy fire escape, clutching the metal railing, his emotions changed. In some strange way, he felt safe out there, safer than he had felt all day. *Funny how something dangerous seems safe when something worse comes along.* He felt far above everything and had a strategic view of the back of all the buildings. No one could jump out at him with a knife from a hidden corner. Open air surrounded him. He could even see the next street over, the same area where he was sure he'd seen Saw earlier that morning.

He remembered when he was growing up that his next-door neighbor had a tree house. He knew he was viewed as a nervous, sickly little boy with asthma, but for a short time the boy next door spent time with him, since there were no other kids on the block. Climbing up the little boards nailed to the tree always made him feel a little queasy, but once he got to the top of the wooden platform, everything was fine. Squid would sit with him in the tree house and eat graham crackers. The cool breezes in the summer and the covering of green leaves all around him made him feel peaceful inside. Somehow he felt safe from the horrible things happening in his own family when he was in the tree house. No adults ever came up there. They usually didn't even know where he was. He didn't have to think about his mom's changing boyfriends or about Sammy. He felt the same way he felt in the tree house as he stood on the fire escape.

Squid thought for a moment about simply staying up on the fire escape. His stomach hurt and his toe was throbbing and he couldn't really think of what to do next. His mind felt like a subway train crowded with too many passengers. He wanted to sit somewhere and think about everything that had happened this morning. He wanted to think about how he was going to kill Larry and get away from Saw and avoid Molly and defend his good name in the park.

But most of all he wanted to think about Rachel and what happened this morning and why his stomach always felt funny when she started talking serious about God and how much he detested Jason. Squid kept hearing Rachel's laugh and seeing her look at him. He felt like he was eight years old and someone had just told him that he would never have a Christmas or a birthday ever again. Sure, his stomach was hurting, but the more he thought about it, the more he figured it wasn't hurting because he was scared of Saw. It was hurting because of something else. It just felt empty.

The day was getting more and more humid, and he was standing in the sun. He could hear Spanish music on someone's radio and kids playing on the next street and cars going up and down the avenues. Squid shook his head and tried to think like a warrior for a moment, and it dawned on him that he could be trapped like a rat on this creaky fire escape. He tried to imagine what he would do if Saw stuck his head out the window right now. Saw was very athletic. His dark biceps bulged when he reached in his pocket and gave Squid the hundred bucks. He could probably be out on that fire escape and at Squid's throat before Squid could even reach for his little bat.

"If I start moving, maybe my stomach won't hurt so bad," he said to himself. He found that if he didn't put pressure on his toe, it didn't hurt him too much. Slowly and deliberately he tested the strength of each section of the railing as he started to descend. Once he started to move, he realized again how much he hated heights. He went past the second floor very quietly and refused to look in any of the windows. At least he couldn't hear any talking there anymore. After he passed the second floor, he stopped for a moment to rest and look around.

He felt safer here. Even if someone came out on the fire escape, his pursuer would have to take his time to get to

Squid. Being high up off the ground didn't seem like such a bad thing after all. "A squirrel is not so dumb," he said as he felt a momentary breeze along the ladder. Squid looked up at the third floor and down at the ground. He wanted Flicker to be safe. He felt an urge to say something out loud to protect her. Like a prayer or something.

Squid felt a dull pain in his stomach. Somehow the life he had yesterday seemed so much sweeter than he had realized. He liked the times of sitting up on the roof of the squat and eating Chinese food and talking to Unc about anything and everything. He liked the fact that he didn't have to worry about mowing the lawn or punching a clock or dressing up or utility bills or car insurance or any of the things that made the Wall Street jerks walk so fast on First Avenue. He liked the fact that there was a little bit of danger in his life, the fact that he and Unc never knew who might jump onto their roof from another abandoned building. He liked having to position himself on the roof to make sure he wasn't a target for some pathetic junkie.

A little bit of real danger was fun. Squid felt sorry for the people in the Disney World advertisements in the baseball magazines. They were having pretend adventures, adventures without risk. Squid was glad he wasn't like them. When it was a good night, when they had a little money and Unc wasn't too drunk, Unc would look up at the sky and point out the few stars they could see above all the lights. Then he'd say, "We're the last Huckleberry Finns! This squat is our raft. We're the richest men in America." As he rested on the ladder, Squid thought maybe Unc was just messing with Squid's mind, the way he did with Jason. When Unc was in a good mood, and he often was, Unc would quote a poem he got from somewhere.

"For those who fight for life," Unc would say, "life has a flavor the protected would never know. That's a little poem, almost like a haiku, Squid. A friend of mine long ago was a fighter pilot. He always kept that poem written on a piece of paper in his pocket. You're like a fighter pilot in your own way, grandson."

Yes, Squid liked a little danger like a weak junkie trying to snitch your pocket change. But he did not want to be a target for someone like Saw and all his goony friends. Saw was a different kind of animal. He did not want to meet Saw with a huge knife in a dark passageway with no one around. Saw was smart enough and mean enough to arrange such a meeting fast. Or Saw could take advantage of Squid wherever Saw found him. Squid shifted his weight to the side and tilted his head to see if he could hear anything from the second floor.

Some crazy woman from a building that wasn't a squat shouted out to him, "I'll call the police!"

"Oh shut up!" he shouted back and kept working his way slowly down. When he got to the bottom rung, he realized that he would have to dangle from the bottom rung of the ladder and then drop a few feet to the ground. He cringed to think what that would do to his toe. Finally, after some lengthy maneuvering, he let go of the iron ladder. Even though he favored his good foot, he still shouted "Ouch!" when he hit the ground. The ground was covered with gravel and broken glass. He was lucky he didn't cut himself too.

Squid dusted himself off and checked to make sure his souvenir bat was still tied securely and hanging straight beneath his pants. Squid looked around him and thought about Jason's little speech at breakfast. Squid was behind an abandoned building along a row of abandoned buildings. Some of the buildings had windows and some did not. Trash, scrap metal, broken glass, and hypodermic needles littered the space. Because visibility was limited, people came through the vacant lot to get here to shoot up, smoke crack, have sex. Squid watched them from the third story sometimes. Battered women, women that looked as bad and worse than Molly, would come back here with men. The women, these junkies, would look so pathetic. They were very thin with tons of wrinkles and sometimes wore makeup that made them look like clowns. They had jerky movements and looked very sick. The men looked like scarecrows or zombies. Squid could only watch them for a moment because the acts they performed together seemed so sad, so mechanical. They looked like soiled, worn-out puppets just going through the motions. It was like some larger, evil puppeteer was making them do all those things. For Squid, it was a horror movie from childhood.

The heat reflecting off the buildings made the little space feel like an oven. Squid thought about showing Jason this enclosed area, this side pocket of broken dreams and nightmares. He doubted that Jason could handle it. Jason probably didn't realize that just a few blocks away from where he talked so righteously about goodness were such nightmarish places. Squid scowled and spit on the gravel. He wondered about those Wall Street businessmen Jason mentioned, working just blocks away. He wondered if they ever thought there were places like this so close by as they worked in their air-conditioned skyscraper offices. "This is what hell is going to be like," Squid said out loud. The air was so thick and humid that his voice hardly seemed to carry a few feet before it dropped to the ground. He gingerly picked his way through the glass toward the vacant lot.

When Squid got to the sidewalk, he found he could walk as long as he kept the pressure on the injured foot's heel. He turned the corner as quickly as he could to avoid being spotted from his own building.

"Squid!" someone shouted behind him.

Not quick enough, Squid thought. For a moment he considered running but knew he would look stupid with his swollen toe. Squid touched the bat on the side of his leg as he turned around. Cheese and Squeaky were pushing their shopping cart toward him. Cheese and Squeaky never looked too intimidating. Cheese was a young kid with reddish brown hair and dark skin. His eyes bulged out a bit, which gave him a constant expression of alarm. Squeaky looked twice his age with dark hair and dark skin, and she looked after Cheese in a matronly way. They lived in a tent in the park and walked around gathering cans and bottles during the day.

They both had a flushed look of excitement that made Squid feel very uncomfortable. Without any other words of greeting, Cheese blurted out, "Saw is looking for you right now, and he says he'll give twenty dollars to anyone who beats you up." In the packed subway of his mind, Squid tried to sort out what this felt like. He found the memory. Cheese and Squeaky looked like two school kids who had the latest news on a fight in the schoolyard. Surely Unc would have some wise comment about some kids being bigger than others. As a child, Squid was often one of the two school kids, forced to be the center of attention against his will. Squid had that same feeling he had as that kid at a new school, when he was being pushed into a fight he did not want to have, egged on by the eager and unfriendly.

Cheese relieved him of the burden of having to say anything. "Squeaky and I used to hate Saw. You know we think he took our dog, Bobo, and did something horrible to him. You know he used to always be bragging about stealing people's pets and sacrificing them on the altar or some other weird garbage like that. I used to think he took Squeaky's cat too."

Squeaky nodded enthusiastically. Cheese continued: "But he's not as bad to us as we used to think he was. At least when he says he'll do something, he does it. Do you want to find him?"

"Yeah," Squid muttered with little conviction.

"He headed that way from the park." Cheese pointed north and asked, "Do you want us to help you find him?" Squeaky nodded again energetically.

Squid kept walking south. "No, I have to take care of some business first. I'll catch up with Saw later. I didn't cheat him."

"If you fight him, make sure he takes that knife off. He's mean with that big knife. If he's not trying to kill you, he likes to try to scar you up as much as he can."

"Thanks, Cheese. I gotta go now." Squid accelerated his limping stride. "I'm no coward," he said in between steps.

Squid limped down the street away from the park, trying to sort out what he should do next. It felt like people were after him—Saw, Molly, maybe Larry, and now whomever else Saw could pay. People in the park didn't like Saw, but they didn't like people who cheated people out of money either. The fact that Saw had gotten the word out to so many people made Squid feel a little creepy. At this point, Squid would just run if he could. He would get on a subway, and he didn't really like subways, and he would just ride to somewhere else. Maybe Coney Island. Just somewhere. But then he thought about seeing Rachel at 4:00 the next morning. He didn't even care if Jason came if only he could see her. Just thinking about it made his chest tingly, as though someone were making more space inside him. Feelings always affected Squid's body and senses, but this seemed both scary and good at the same time.

The noon bells went off at the Catholic church as he walked by. It felt like the sounds were banging against his rib cage, inside his heart, cleaning him out. The golden touch of the bell tones inside of him were working in a good way, like spring cleaning. He couldn't leave. Not when he would see Rachel.

What if I just gave Saw the money back? Squid thought. Unc was always telling him that Squid's ability to make good choices in life was somewhat limited and that was why Squid lived in a squat. Squid stopped on the street and tried to be businesslike. He tried to think how he would get the money back to Saw. *I could give the money to Ratchet and Ratchet could give it to him.* Squid didn't know if he could really trust Ratchet with a hundred dollars, but he was the only person Squid could come up with. Unc could be unpredictable when it came to money. For a brief moment, Squid felt a false wave of relief, as if he had a plan, until he remembered that he didn't have a hundred dollars.

Squid groaned out loud and a man on a bike covered with Puerto Rican flags and horns stared at him. The man grinned and showed a mouthful of golden teeth. Then he reached down and turned on the radio that was roped to his bicycle. Salsa music flooded the sidewalk. Squid turned his back to him and closed his eyes and tried to be grown up. Squid couldn't think of anyone he knew who had a hundred dollars, and he would rather die than breathe a word about it to Rachel, or to Jason, for that matter.

Maybe he could get a job and earn the money fast. But Squid just couldn't think of a way to get a job. At this point, he couldn't even walk into a regular store without getting cold stares and the threat of being ejected. He couldn't stand it. He knew he smelled a little bit, not a lot, and he bit his thumbs and wrapped his hands in the front of his shirt, and that he wasn't always clean-shaven. He couldn't think of anyone who might even consider hiring him.

As a child, he remembered going into nice stores and not even thinking about it. Still, sometimes at night in the squat, to help him go to sleep, he would think about going to Yankee Stadium and somehow getting into the locker room and shaking hands with Don Mattingly. If he still couldn't go to sleep, he'd think about hitting that home run and hearing people shout. Then he'd pretend that Don asked him to come live in his home and to help him practice. Then Don would take care of all his problems.

I know, he thought, *I'll beg for the money. I'll do what Unc does. Someone will give me a hundred dollars.* Unc was probably sitting right now on one of his favorite street corners, wrapped in a sheet and reading some old paperback book by someone from a thousand years ago. He would have a paper cup in front of it and put some change or a dollar bill in it so that anyone who came by could drop something in. Unc had told him to always be good-natured, to say thank you or God bless you no matter what, even if the person curses. In fact, if someone curses, respond with a kind word, because the person behind him might feel sorry about it. That was often the way Unc got money to buy a bottle, if Squid did not give him enough. The key was to continue to be good-natured, no matter how insulting or humiliating the person was who went by.

Squid did not have a gift for being good-natured and had never begged. He just got his mental disability check and spent it on Chinese food and dope and maybe some magazine about the Yankees. Then he gave some to Unc. When he ran out, he just scrounged around at the missions until he got another check.

But Squid was ready to beg today. He had heard guys in the park brag about having a lucky day at Times Square and getting two hundred dollars in a day. All he needed was half that amount. Maybe this was his day to make a lucky swing and hit a home run. Unc never got that much because he stayed on the poorer streets in his own neighborhood. But as he walked, Squid determined to go over to First Avenue and get a hundred dollars. First Avenue had a lot more traffic with a lot more people with money. He wished Unc were there to advise him. It was the best plan he could come up with on his own.

Squid rarely left the group of blocks that were his neighborhood. Staying in his own group of about ten blocks wasn't all that great, but at least it made him feel safe. It was probably the way Unc must feel surrounded by his bundle of dirty blankets. The last time Squid left the area was to go visit Unc on "the Raft" when Unc got in trouble. Visiting Unc was not enjoyable, and the experience kept him from going outside his block anymore.

From time to time the cops would come to Squid's neighborhood and do a "sweep." They said they didn't do that kind of thing, but they did. They'd hit a corner where there was a lot of drug activity and just pick up every person on the corner. It was like pulling in a whole bunch of fish in a net to get the good ones. Most of the ones who hadn't done anything would be released from central booking in forty-eight hours. But forty-eight hours was a long time in central booking.

Unc was on the corner buying a bottle when the police did a sweep. Squid didn't know why but somehow Unc didn't get out in forty-eight hours. He ended up in a place called the Raft. Unc never would explain why. Squid had heard about it. It was a big barge in Queens where prisoners were kept. Unc called the mission to let Squid know where he was. Squid left to get him.

Squid hadn't taken a subway for awhile, but it wasn't so bad. He found an empty seat and tried to make himself as small as possible. The person sitting next to him on the bench got up and stood by the door. Squid knew he didn't smell great and getting clean clothes was always a problem. He had to ride the subway a long way and then take a bus. On the bus he started passing warehouses and big spaces surrounded by old chain-link fences. He felt as though he had sat on the bus, biting his thumbs, forever. He had to change buses. He stood for a long time next to the dismal bus sign in front of a weedy lot.

"Where you going, kid!" an old man shouted to him as he dragged some old corrugated metal down the street.

"To, to the jail . . . the Raft, I mean," Squid stuttered.

"You're at the wrong bus stop, guy. That one is over there." The old man freed up one of his hands and pointed across the street.

Squid crossed the street and touched the curb three times with his foot. When he was a little boy, Squid loved to be with people sometimes. But that was a long time ago. He felt that knot in his stomach forming as he got closer to the jail. He wiped his wet hands on his shirt.

On the next bus, the bus driver showed him where to get off with a bored nod of his head. Squid found himself in a place with a lot of butcher warehouses and empty lots with tall grass. It wasn't all packed in like it was in the Lower East Side. Squid looked around for a sign to tell him where the barge was. Nothing. He looked around for someone to ask. Nobody. He'd been living in squats long enough to know that standing alone out there among the warehouses made him a target. Finally Squid saw an older Hispanic woman walking toward some fences with razor wire on the top. A gust of wind picked up dust and blew it in his eyes. There weren't any buildings around to protect him.

Squid followed the woman and went through a maze of chain-link fences and razor wire. He could see the Raft in the distance. Finally he came up to a huge gray door. A sign said you could not have any jewelry or metal objects on when you visited a prisoner. The lady he had followed buzzed the buzzer. A big guard, a woman, opened the door and let her right in. The door shut again in Squid's face.

"No panic attacks, now," Squid said to himself to keep up his nerve. He sucked up his courage and buzzed the buzzer, and the guard came to the door. She looked Squid up and down as if Squid were a bag of trash.

"No jewelry admitted," she said brusquely and shut the door again.

Squid leaned his hand against the chain-link fence as if to say to anyone watching, "I meant for that to happen." He was all alone outside the door. No one was watching. Squid stood motionless, looking around to see if there was a sign that explained what he needed to do next. Nothing. He was paralyzed, wanting equally to give up and take the long bus ride and train ride back home and wanting to see Unc. Finally he buzzed the buzzer again.

The woman, as big as an ox, opened the door again, obviously irritated at the trouble she was going through. She looked at Squid and said nothing.

"Please, madam, I mean ma'am, officer, . . . please, your honor, this is the first time I have ever come and I didn't know that you couldn't wear jewelry. I came all the way from Lower Manhattan. It took me a half a day to get here. What do I do now to see my friend?"

"Sorry, no jewelry inside." She slammed the door.

"Wait, wait, wait. Isn't there something I could do?" Squid was once again staring at a door. He went along the fence and sat down. "I'm not leaving until I see Unc."

"Hey, you, you can't sit there. Get moving." Another officer approached from the other side and startled Squid. He jumped like a cat.

"Please, sir, mister, reverend, uh, officer, I just want to get inside, but the lady said that I couldn't wear jewelry. What do I do? I gotta see my friend."

"You take it over to the main office and put it in a locker for a quarter like everybody else has to! Now move on."

"Now why couldn't the first guard have told me that?" he said, but the guard had already moved on.

As Squid waited in line at the front desk in the main office, he dug in all his pockets, searching for a quarter, checking each pocket over and over again. His forehead was all sweaty and he tried not to bite his lips. When he finally made it to the front of the line, he looked at the clerk with pleading eyes. "Look, lady, I've never been here before and I didn't know you had to bring quarters. What should I do?" The lady looked at Squid for a long time with a blank look, as if Squid were nothing, a zero. The people in line behind Squid began to shuffle around impatiently. The silence was unbearable for him. He bit his thumb to keep from whimpering.

Finally the clerk rolled her eyes and pulled a change purse out of her pocket. She handed him a quarter, pointed to the lockers, and without changing expressions, turned to the next person in line. "Next," she said.

Squid put his bracelet in a locker and returned to the big door. "Why is everyone making this so hard?" he said to himself as he braced himself to face the abrupt guard at the visitors door. The guard opened the door and looked at Squid with a passive face. She didn't give a hint of recognition or utter a syllable of apology. This time she let him in. He entered and glared at her.

"Get your shoes and belt on the table. Hurry up!"

Squid was shocked but moved as quickly as he could. His pants were pretty loose without his belt and he had to hold one side of them to keep them up.

"Wait over here."

Squid hustled to the corner where some other people were standing.

"No, over here!" another guard called. "Make sure your pockets are completely empty."

The group of people—a girlfriend, Squid supposed, a mother, and an older man—all shuffled over to the new post.

"Put shoelaces, hair bands, and belts over there."

"Over where?" Squid asked.

A woman who had been there before simply said, "Over where those lockers are." The place looked a little like Squid's junior high school locker room.

Squid hurried over to the second set of lockers and put up his shoes and his belt. "Anybody got another quarter? This is my first time here and I didn't know about all this."

"Here," a woman in her twenties gave him a quarter. "They don't have to be like this, you know. It's like they want to make this feel like a concentration camp. This is my first time here. I don't belong in a place like this. They don't have to treat us like criminals. We're not. We may be visiting criminals, but we're not criminals."

"Yeah," Squid said as he locked his second locker and dug through all his pockets, trying to remember where he put his first set of keys. Finally he found it, and he put his second set of keys with it. He stopped and made a conscious effort to remember in which pocket he had put the keys. He looked down at the front of his shirt. He was embarrassed to see that he had a ring of sweat around each armpit. "What do we do now?" he asked the lady as they sat down in a row of chairs.

"I don't know. They could have told us, you know. They don't have to play mind games with us and make us so uncertain."

Squid sat next to her in silence for a long time. Finally another guard motioned for them to go through another metal detector. "Take your shoes off," the guard barked. Squid held his pants and stepped through in his stocking feet. He tried to cover the hole that let his big toe stick out. His big toe looked obscene. When he got through, he sat down in another row of chairs.

After arguing with the guard, the lady came and sat by Squid again. "They don't have to make us feel this way, you know. They take our clothes and dignity and make us feel like we're heading for the showers in a concentration camp. If the guards would just use a little courtesy, if they would just look you in the eye every once in awhile . . ."

"I'm not going to say anything because I'm afraid they won't let me see my friend," Squid finally said quietly.

The older lady sitting across from them began to cry.

"What's wrong, lady? You don't speak English? Whatchoo cryin' about?" Another large guard, a woman with a booming voice, stood over her.

"She says you have been making fun of her and she is going to report you," the younger woman sitting next to Squid said.

The guard stuck her chin out. "Let her report me. I don't care. If people would just learn a little *English*, they wouldn't have that problem." She marched back to the metal detector.

Squid squeezed his hands really hard to keep from lunging at the guard. The lady next to him was called to crowd in a smaller room, but Squid had to wait longer in the waiting room. *Maybe they're not going to let me in because I didn't follow instructions quick enough,* Squid thought. *Maybe it's because I made a bad face at the first guard at the door. Maybe the guard at the door called ahead about me, and they are going to make fun of me and make me wait the entire day. Maybe it's a trap, and they are going to let all the visitors go in and then they are going to keep me here. Why does that guard not ever look at me? Just look at me one time, like I'm a person. I'm not a criminal. I'm somebody. I got a name. Why are they treating us like we are animals?*

Finally Squid was motioned into the next room. "Fill out these forms," another guard said. She tossed a pencil in Squid's direction and shoved a card and a yellow paper toward him. The guard with the papers looked at the other guard and rolled her eyes. Squid didn't miss the look. He picked up the pencil, dropped it on the floor, then hurried to pick it up. He quickly brought the pencil up again but hit it on the table as he was coming up. The pencil hit the floor again. The guard with the papers twittered and exchanged glances with the other guard. She wrinkled up her nose. "Does your home have a shower?"

"What?"

"Does your home have a shower?" The other guard put her hand over her mouth and snickered.

"That's none of your business," Squid said quietly.

"What did you say?" The guard acted indignant. "State your full name and address here," she said and motioned at the papers.

"You want to know my full name? This is my full name." Squid broke the pencil in two with a snap and held half the pencil where the lead was sticking out. He held it in his fist and printed in big block letters across the form *SQUID*.

"And here is my full, full address. S-Q-U-A-T. That's who I am. That's where I live. That's all you're allowed to know." He threw the papers in the air and slammed the broken pencil on the desk. He stomped out of the room and past the woman at the metal detector site then past the lockers and the people there looking scared and waiting for instructions. He stomped to the first metal detector and the woman at the door. He looked up at the guard at the door and said, "I'm Squid, that's who I am." He stood and looked her in the eye for a moment, then he remembered he didn't have his belt or his shoelaces.

Squid looked down at the ground. He wanted to see Unc. He wanted to be loyal to his friend. "I'm sorry," he muttered to the mean guard at the door. The guard looked at him in icy silence. He trudged back through the second metal detector and sat down and waited in line again to get in to see Unc. In silence, the guards exchanged looks.

He pulled some wadded ID papers out of his pocket. After talking to several guards and finally the captain, he was allowed to fill out the forms again. He didn't know why, but he changed some letters in his name and the numbers in his address as he filled out the form. Nobody noticed. Eventually he was ushered to the next waiting room. He knew the guards made him wait a lot longer than everyone else, but finally he got in to see Unc.

He was given a stamp on his hand and then a door on the other side of the room opened. Squid was released into a huge room where all the men wore orange overalls. Woman with children, mothers of prisoners, and friends were chatting with prisoners over little round Formica tables bolted to the floor.

There was Unc, grinning and looking a little sickly, holding his hand out graciously to Squid. Unc's bright orange coveralls made his skin seem even more wrinkled and old.

"Unc, why do they treat people like that? We're just the visitors. We're not even prisoners. But they do everything they can, they go out of their way to make us feel like dirt, like garbage."

"You just have to be philosophic about these things, Squid. Look at me, I'm a prisoner, and my crime was going to the store at the wrong time. But you just have to get some distance from these things. You know, for every bad guard, there are thirty that are pretty decent fellows. They have families. They joke around with us. Just like Boethius said. There are ups and downs. A wheel of fortune. Highs and lows."

"How can you be so cheerful? This has got to be a new low. Speaking of highs and lows, that's another thing, Unc. How come you're the only white guy here in a room with a hundred prisoners?" Squid motioned with his head to the other people in the room. "How come every single other person is black or Hispanic or has darker skin like me. Are you telling me no white people are doing crimes? That doesn't make sense."

"Ah Squid, blind justice is not so blind," Unc said amiably. "And since we are thinking of what affects justice, were you able to deposit a little money for me here? It is a wretched experience being anywhere with no money, even on this raft. And I'm not feeling much like Huckleberry Finn today."

Squid moved out of his memory, still thinking about Unc as he left his familiar area to go make some money for Saw. He wondered how the prison guards would have treated someone like Jason the jerk. Would they have treated him the same way they treated Squid? He doubled up his fists and walked with determination toward First Avenue.

A young man with a crisp white shirt bumped into him. The man looked right through Squid without a word of apology or change of expression. Squid remembered again the way the prison guards treated him and felt a rush of nervousness whip through his stomach. Why did he feel so scared and then so angry? It was really worse than fearing being beaten up by a bunch of stupid junkies looking for twenty dollars or fearing that someone would rob him.

Squid knew that taxis wouldn't even take people to his own area, but he would rather be there than on First Avenue. Squid didn't really feel all that comfortable with people he didn't know, and here he was going to ask total strangers for money. He shrugged his shoulders. He didn't know what else to do, so he was going for it. He saw a paper cup in the trash can on the corner and pulled it out. He thought of Unc and said out loud, "Like a warrior."

All the avenues in Squid's area didn't really seem to lead anywhere, but First Avenue led all the way to Wall Street. Most of the people around the park in his neighborhood were artists or punks or people who looked like they shopped at the Salvation Army or a mission clothing-closet. But when someone approached First Avenue, the world changed. People wore suits and dresses, walked with purpose, and looked at their watches. They had beautiful teeth. Squid always felt as though he were going to another country when he got to First Avenue. Though pushy men and women stood on the corners of First Avenue and shouted out the name of the drug they were selling, Squid figured they did this so that people from the suburbs could buy something without having to go into the squats area.

Squid sat down on a stretch of the wall next to a newsstand. He rested his back against the brick. He was very tired of walking on his heel so that his toe wouldn't hurt. He put his paper cup out in front of him and waited. Nothing. He wished there were some kind of street tree or something next to the newsstand. The place was an oven. He waited some more. Not one person even looked at him. They walked by in their nice suits and pretty outfits and looked right past him. Anger bubbled up in Squid's throat. He wanted to shout, "Hey! Look me in the eyes. I've got things to do too. I've got friends too. I've got Unc and Ratchet and Rachel. I'm not a zero!" That's what Squid felt like as he sat up against the brick wall. He felt like he was dead, like he was a ghost. He felt that no matter what he did or said, no one would look at him. It was like that play they did in his junior high school before he left, when the dead people came back to their own place and they saw how wonderful everything was. Squid felt like one of those dead people that nobody saw. But in the play, when those characters looked back on life, they felt like life was wonderful. Squid didn't feel like life was so wonderful.

He pulled a dollar bill out and put it in the cup. Unc had told him that putting money in the cup was absolutely necessary. He knew that most beggars on First Avenue would shout out something like, "Can you spare some change, sir?" or "Do you have some money for some food, ma'am?" Or even "Could you help me buy a bus ticket to get home?" But he absolutely could not do that; he felt way too uncomfortable to do that. For a brief moment, he thought about holding his mom's hand long ago and getting into a car to go to the store with her on a bright, happy day. If she had had it, she would've given him some change to buy a Butterfinger candy bar. What would his mom say if she saw him now, dirty and desperate? Would she still pat him on the head and look at him with her wide eyes? Would she tell him he was such a big man now? Squid pushed the thought down and started looking at his shoes. He took his right shoe off to look at his toe. Maybe someone would look at his black and blue toe and feel sorry for him. Not a chance.

"Hey, Squid."

CHAPTER 7

SQUID LOOKED UP. It was Jason. Of all people. Squid's face grew flushed. He looked at how far away Jason was standing on the sidewalk and thought he could reach out with his good foot and clip Jason behind his knee and make him fall on the sidewalk in front of all these people with business suits on. That would embarrass him.

"Hi," Squid finally said in a monotone. He didn't look at Jason's face. He kept staring at his knees.

It looked as though Jason felt awkward too. "Um, I've got to go over to the hardware store and buy a plunger because the men's toilet is stopped up." Jason smiled as the silence continued. "Top-level assignment."

Squid was acutely aware that his own pants were kind of dirty, that he was sitting and Jason was standing, that Jason was blond and tan and had such white teeth. "Why don't you just keep walking until you get down to Wall Street," Squid suggested. "You'll feel more at home down there."

Jason had to step closer to Squid because he was blocking the way for other people moving purposefully on the street. "Yeah, maybe I would," he replied.

Squid looked down the street and refused to look Jason in the face.

Jason reached in his pocket awkwardly and squatted down to look Squid in the eye. "But today I think I'm going to invest in someone who could be a new friend." Jason stuffed two one-dollar bills into Squid's paper cup. Jason smiled almost nervously and stood up. "See you at four in the morning. I'm off on my mission to flush out sewage for humanity."

"Yeah," was all Squid could say as Jason walked off down the street. Why did the one person he despised have to be the one person who treated him kindly? Why was Jason the only person who looked him in the eye, even on First Avenue? Squid took the two dollars Jason had put in his cup and the dollar bill he had put in. *I've been here over a half hour and I made two dollars,* Squid said to himself. *Let's see, how long would it take me to make a hundred dollars at that rate? More than ten hours? That's going to take some hard computing.*

As Squid sat in the heat and tried to think like a businessman again, he realized he had enough to buy some squid at his favorite Chinese takeout. He found four more dollars in his back pocket that he had forgotten about. The Chinese takeout wasn't that far away, and with some food in his stomach, he could decide what he should do next.

Squid decided to wait a little longer there on the sidewalk. Not a tree was planted on this sidewalk. A few spaces, where trees once were, dotted the path like the black squares in a crossword puzzle. Dogs did their business in these spaces now. Cars on the avenue and air conditioners hanging out of windows did their business in the air, cranking up the temperature.

It was so hot. Squid could hardly sit on the sidewalk. "Help me, sir," he called out to one young man who actually looked at him. "I'm sizzlin' in a frying pan here."

"Get a job!" the man shouted as he kept walking.

"Yeah, you get a job!" Squid shouted back. If only he could say something smart like Unc could.

Squid pretended he had landed on Mars. He had to wait right here, no matter how hot it got, until the mother ship returned. Every minute felt like a day. "I'm dying. I'm on a hot plate here," he radioed to his fellow astronauts in their air-conditioned control room in their hover pod. "We're talking overcooked hot dog on a grill."

No one gave him any money. He was just street furniture, like a fire hydrant. "Hey, look at me!" he shouted to a woman with a crisp purple dress and lots of perfume. She didn't even break her stride.

"I'll look at you."

Squid looked up. A Hispanic man with a briefcase was standing right next to him. He had curly hair and smelled like cologne. His head blocked out the sun so that Squid couldn't see him too well. He stood there for a long time without saying a word. "You know, you can do better than this. You are a strong young man. You don't have to be begging."

"Yeah, right. Thanks for the sermon, mister. What do you know about my life anyway? You don't have a clue about what my life is like."

"Look at me, man. I'm Puerto Rican. I've got a suit on, but I grew up on Ave D. I used to deal on Ave C. Why should I give money to a man who looks younger and stronger than I am?"

"Look, sir, I don't have time for this. I'm in deep trouble and I need to get a hundred bucks today. If you don't have any ideas about how to do that, let's just not waste each other's time." Squid purposely looked at another passerby. "Any spare change?" he shouted.

"Look, man, I used to have a hard time too. But now I'm not only a teacher, I'm the principal of the grade school on Sixth Street over there. This is what I always tell the kids and this is what I've learned. The rich are rich because they do what they say they will do. They keep their promises. Their word is good. Because of that, their name is good. When they say something, you can depend on it. That is why they are rich. So start a habit of doing exactly what you say you are going to do. And do it on time. Do it exactly on time. When you say you will show up, show up at exactly the right *minute*. That's what I tell all my kids."

"Thanks a lot. Look, sir, I'm probably going to get killed today. I'm probably going to have my scalp removed and hung out the window of a squat, and you're giving me this little Sunday school lecture about being on time."

The man put his briefcase down and squatted by Squid

as if he had something important to say. "I'll tell you what I'll do . . . uh . . . what's your name?"

Squid narrowed his eyes. "Why do you want to know?"

"Stop playing around with me, man, and tell me your name."

Squid looked down at the sidewalk. "It's Squid."

"Squid? Right. You'll get lots of jobs with that name. Listen, Squid, I'll make a deal with you so that you can make a hundred dollars. Today."

"Don't make fun of me, sir. I'm having a really rough day."

"No, no, I'm serious, but you have to follow my instructions exactly or I won't give you anything. No exceptions. Look, I've got to run an errand, but I will be coming down Ave A in a half hour. I'll be heading toward the school. Where can I pick you up?"

Squid looked at him with suspicion. "At the Chinese takeout place close to Sixth Street," he blurted.

"Right," the man continued. "I'll come by and pick you up there at exactly, exactly, 1:30 p.m. If you're not there at exactly 1:30 p.m., the deal is off. No excuses, no exceptions. If you're not there, you'll have shown me you're another slug that's too lazy to do anything. But if you are there, I will take you to the school and give you a broom and you can sweep and clean the sidewalk and the fences all the way around the school. The janitors will not be there, so they will never know. If you work eight hours straight until 9:30 p.m., I'll give you a hundred bucks cash out of my own pocket. I'll give it to you today."

Squid got up from the sidewalk and balanced himself on his knees. "You're not kidding with me, sir, are you? You're not teasing me? Because if you'll do that, it might save my life. I'll do anything. I'm a good worker. I'll do whatever you say."

"Just remember, 1:30 sharp at the Chinese takeout. No excuses. Not a minute later. That's why street people don't get jobs. They don't understand about time. See you." The man in the suit marched with purpose around the corner.

Peace welled up inside Squid like helium. "I'm going to get the money today. I'll get it back to Saw somehow. Ratchet will help me. I'm going to live. Everything will be like it was before. Things have a way of working out." Slowly and carefully he picked the money out of the cup and put it in his pocket. A man came out of the store and hit Squid with the side of his broom as if he were sweeping him away.

"Getta outa the fronta my store," he said very quickly with a funny accent. "No bums ina fronta my store. Get out! You stink like trash!" He hit Squid again with the broom. Squid grabbed the broom. The man yanked on the broom but couldn't get it away from Squid. For a brief moment, their eyes locked. Squid was getting ready to swing his leg around and kick the man in the knee. But he was in the man's territory, not his own, and he had a hundred dollars waiting for him. He stood up slowly, holding onto the broom and staring at the man.

"You're nothing butta garbage," the storeowner said. Squid was standing now. He let go of the broom and backed away, staring at the man. He turned the corner toward his own neighborhood.

Squid had little time to waste. *I'll go to the Chinese place now, get something to eat, and make sure I'm there on time.* He chose a way to get to the restaurant that would keep him the furthest from the park. "Just eight more hours and things will be better," he said. "I'll show that guy how hard I can work."

The Chinese takeout was a dirty little storefront with a faded sign with Chinese and English characters on it. The place was old enough that Squid didn't feel embarrassed to go in. Everything had a kind of greasy film on it. The radio was always blaring Chinese music and something was always sizzling on one of the woks they had behind the counter. A dirty ceiling fan disturbed the thick air, and the skinny cook always had a cigarette dangling out of his mouth. The large older lady at the counter did not know English, but she knew Squid and knew that he always ordered the same thing. She nodded when he came in, and he sat down at one of the tables to wait.

When his meal was ready—pieces of squid in sauce in a tinfoil plate, no drink—he sat down again. Before he started eating, he closed his eyes and counted, "One, two, three. One, two, three. One, two, three." Three times three times three. Twenty-seven times. As he ate, he began to relax. He looked dreamily out the window. His whole body felt so sleepy. He looked at the clock covered with film, hanging next to the menus on the wall. He still had twenty minutes with nothing to do. He had better not eat too fast. That was

the problem with his life now. Even on a day when he had
to think like a warrior and he felt he was being chased by
an army of evil-wishers, there were still these long stretches
of time when he just had to wait.

Somehow it was different when Squid was a child.
Even with all the terrible things that he would never speak
about or even think about or dream about, even with all
that, he remembered in the better times having toys and
watching TV and going to appointments in the car with
his mom. People seemed to be doing things. They had a
purpose. But now, usually there was no place to go. There
was no money, no TV, no work, nobody you really wanted
to see. The hours just went on and on. Time just stretched
out like Chinese noodles.

Squid looked at the clock again. His food was gone,
and he was lost in a daydream. Fifteen minutes had passed.
No wonder Squid looked forward to weed when he had the
money, and no wonder people drank just to get through
the night or did the other drugs. Squid didn't touch those
harder drugs because he was so scared of them, but no wonder people did them. It was just so boring. At least Squid
had made two dollars and he had something to do. And for
once he had someone coming by to meet him. He could sit
at this table and watch through the window as people just
walked by. Squid didn't have to think about anything. He
had time to spare before the man came.

Squid looked up at the fan that was turning above him.
Every time it went around, it knocked. Little gray pieces of
fuzz were stuck along the edges. Squid began to feel that

pieces of fuzz were dropping into his meal, so he moved his plate over. He made sure the edges of his tinfoil plate were parallel to the edges of the table. He looked over at the display window at the counter. The glass was so foggy with grease he could hardly see what was inside. He remembered a time of reaching up with his hands to place them on a display window. It was his birthday. He was eleven years old.

"You can choose any kind of ice cream you want today, sweetie," his mom had said as she stroked the back of his head. "There's thirty-one flavors, you know. This day is just for you and me. You are my date for the day." Her eyes got wide and made him think that the day would last forever. "Just choose whatever, whatever you want. Anything."

"Could I have that rainbow ice cream with all the different flavors, please? That's my favorite, Mom, especially on a hot day like today. And could I have a scoop of tangerine flavor? Yeah, that one over there. Can I taste that lime over there? Thank you. Yes, I want a lime scoop on top. Yes, I can balance it. What do you want, Mom?"

"I think I'm just going to sit across from you and watch you eat, honey. That's the best treat I could think of." She pulled out her little change purse and brought a wadded-up dollar bill out and spread it out on the counter. Then she pulled out some quarters and pennies and counted them out one by one. The ice cream man balanced the triple scoop ice cream cone in one hand and waited patiently. His mom continued to count, separating the quarters and pennies into groups. The ice cream store seemed very quiet. She looked up at the man and gave him a nervous smile.

"That should be enough," he said, not changing his expression.

"Oh, you are too kind," his mom gushed. "It's his birthday you know."

"I know. I heard."

"You're becoming such a big man now," his mom said as they sat on the plastic bench. The Formica of the table felt so cool as he worked on the top scoop of lime ice cream. His mom put the small change purse back in her regular purse. She always wore more makeup than the other people's moms, but somehow it looked good on her. "Who cares if the other kids at school have other things to do," she said as she snapped her purse shut. "It's their loss."

His mom had gotten a straw at the counter and a small cup of water. "Look at this." She ripped off the top of the straw wrapper and pushed the rest of the wrapping to the bottom of the straw. She pulled the straw out and left the wrapping all wrinkled and compressed in a knot. She put the straw in the cup of water and put her fingertip on the top. "Watch this," she said and suspended the straw over the mashed wrapper. She released a drop of water onto the wrapping. Like magic, the wrapper began to unwind and move on its own. It looked as if it were alive. She released another couple of drops until the entire wrapping had no wrinkles. From a little knot, it had stretched out full length. It was a miracle.

His mouth formed a perfect O of wonder. "Whoa," he whispered.

The lime scoop was almost done when he looked back over to the display window of the counter. Every color of ice cream was placed in neat cardboard buckets in a long line—chocolate, cherry, raspberry, banana. Everything was so neat and clean. The expressionless man behind the counter had a white apron on and not even a smudge of ice cream on him anywhere. How did he do that? Squid and his mom were the only customers in the store. Everything was quiet except for the soft blowing of cool air out of the ducts. He felt so peaceful and clean. It was like a holy place. The plastic seat where he sat across from his mom was so cool to the touch. Nothing could hurt it, even if you dropped ice cream on it. "I like it here, Mom. Let's stay here and never go anywhere else. We could eat ice cream all the time and never be hot."

His mom had touched his hand and smiled in that way she had of smiling, which made him think that anything was possible. "I like it here too, sweetie. We can stay here as long as you want. Forever if you want to. It's your birthday, you know."

A little grease from the wok splashed across the counter and dripped on the glass as the vegetables hissed in the heat. When Squid finished his meal, he kept pushing the last little piece of squid around the tinfoil. The fan above him was still knocking every time it went around. He kept himself from looking but finally checked out the clock again. One twenty-eight. Almost time.

Squid's eyes moved from the clock to the window. As he gazed out the glass, one of the faces stopped in front of the window and turned and looked through the window right at Squid. Was it the man? No, it was a woman's face, haggard, lined, with a sunken nose that had been broken many times. It was Molly, Saw's girlfriend or slave or whatever she was. For a few moments, Squid and Molly simply stared at each other, neither moving. Molly's hair was standing up as if she had just gotten up. She looked like a witch. Then Molly immediately turned and went back the way she had come.

Squid left his meal and bolted out the door and limped in the opposite direction. He didn't even take the time to look in the direction Molly had headed. He was too scared that Saw was right there. Squid would rather Saw put that big knife in his back than face him and thrust it into his stomach. He didn't look back. He turned the first corner at full speed, crossed the street, and finally scurried behind a plywood barrier that jutted onto the sidewalk in front of a building being gutted. He didn't see anyone, so he kept going, making sure he was behind plywood or cars or trees or anything that would block someone's vision as they looked down the street.

Squid kept zigzagging down a few more streets and then slowed to a walk. He was scared. He was mad at himself for running. He was mad at Saw for making his neighborhood a place where nothing went right. He felt like some little animal, like a squirrel or something, on the run from a bunch of crazy dogs that were chasing him and yelping for no good reason except that it was fun. And those dogs didn't care a bit and would tear him to bits if they caught him, and they wouldn't even remember it afterward. Squid started thinking about where he was and began walking more slowly and casually since he knew he looked crazy, running and limping and looking back.

Squid thought about the man with the briefcase. He walked a little further until he could see the clock on the tower. It was already past 1:30. "Ahhh, man." Squid bit down hard on his thumb.

Squid turned another corner and started walking past a big empty lot next to an abandoned high school. In Squid's eyes, the high school looked so lonely and sad with its windows broken out and the doors boarded up. This school was useless. It was not the school he had hoped to be working at, sweeping industriously and finding solutions for his life. The lot next to it looked like a wasteland, a big sandy desert on this hot humid day with broken glass and cans scattered around. And there, on the far side of the lot, to Squid's utter irritation, was a solitary figure. It was Bonehead. Why wasn't Bonehead in the park? Why did he always show up where Squid was? Did he follow Squid around and show up all over the place to annoy him?

And sure enough, there was Bonehead doing the only thing he knew how to do. He was throwing rocks up in the air and hitting them with the same stick he had this morning. He would throw up each rock and whack it with precision at least thirty or forty yards. Squid could hear the solid sound of the stick hitting the rock all the way across the lot. Bonehead saw Squid and turned to hit the rocks in the opposite direction.

Squid marched and limped up to Bonehead to chew him out for he didn't know what. Somehow all of this was

Bonehead's fault. Bonehead scared him half to death this morning by grabbing him from behind. If Bonehead hadn't been there, maybe Squid would have found Saw at dawn and gotten a clear shot with his bat and put an end to all this. Bonehead had the nerve to enter his squat without permission and scared the fear of God out of him by walking around whacking rats. Then Bonehead had the disrespect to snoop around close to where he kept his special envelope that nobody, nobody knew about. It was Bonehead's fault that he was limping with a toe that was black and blue. If he hadn't been limping, maybe he could have gotten back in time to get that job. The heat and Bonehead and this godforsaken vacant lot made Squid snort through his nose in fury.

As Squid got closer, Bonehead threw up another rock to hit another homer away from Squid. For once, he didn't hit it solidly. Instead of going forward, the rock skipped backward in a neat arc and hit Squid smartly on the forehead. Squid moved like lightning and grabbed Bonehead's right hand, which was still holding the stick. With his free forearm, he struck Bonehead in the upper chest and pushed him in a rush against an old chain-link fence. The fence gave a bit, but Squid had him pinned tight. All of a sudden, Squid had all the energy he had been missing. He felt his forearm slide up from Bonehead's chest to his neck. He wanted to give Bonehead a good scare. Bonehead grabbed Squid's elbow with his free hand. Squid pressed hard against Bonehead's neck. Somehow, instead of letting up, Squid's rage surged through his arms and he pressed harder and harder. It felt like someone had pushed his gas pedal to the floor.

At the same time, Bonehead looked Squid in the eye and pushed back on his elbow with a firm grip. In the midday heat, Bonehead's brown face looked huge and sweaty and puzzled. Bonehead was small, but Squid was surprised at how strong he was.

For a brief moment in the heat, all alone in a lot, the two stood pushing with equal pressure on the other. Squid suddenly wasn't sure why he was pressing against Bonehead's neck as hard as he could. He just kept doing it. He pushed harder and pressed his whole body into it. Bonehead pushed back.

At that moment, Squid heard a wild, tiny shriek. It was so close that Squid felt like it was coming from his own churning chest. He was so startled, he let up on Bonehead's neck. *What was that?* It sounded like a tiny human, three inches tall, screaming for help. Squid stepped back and tried to find the source of the scream. There it was, sticking out of Bonehead's shirt pocket. It was that little baby squirrel, screaming her little head off. Squid had never heard anything like it.

Squid was breathing hard and sweat was rolling down his face. "I didn't know a squirrel could sound like that," Squid finally said. Bonehead was rubbing his windpipe and the front part of his neck. "Look, Bonehead, I, um, I'm sorry I hurt your neck. I don't know what got into me. I'm just really having a crazy day, and I don't know what's going on."

The little squirrel was quiet now and hid herself completely in Bonehead's pocket. "Look, Flicker, I'm sorry I scared you too." Squid started rubbing his forehead vigorously in the place that the rock hit him. "But I swear to you, Bonehead, if you hit me with a rock or a stick or anything else today, I'm not going to be responsible for what I do to you."

"Okayokayokay," Bonehead said but sounded hoarse.

Squid feared he had really hurt him and tried to be more gentle. "Did you get Flicker to eat anything more?"

Bonehead kept feeling his neck and didn't answer for awhile. Finally he said, "Gotchamilkaliddle."

"Yeah? Look at her. She's not shivering anymore. She looks like she really likes riding around in your pocket. It must make her feel protected." Squid reached out slowly and gently touched the top of the squirrel's head. "Flicker has more hair than I thought. Maybe it was just all matted down this morning. Look at her, Bonehead, she is pulling up on your shirt like she's climbing a tree." Squid looked around at the lot. "Man, it is hot here." The lot felt lonely and oppressive. It was like he was standing on Mars again. "Look, Bonehead, this is kind of a strange day for me. What do you say I go do my errands and I meet you in the park in half an hour?"

Bonehead gave Squid a puzzled look then dutifully picked up his stick and started walking toward the park.

"Good-bye, Flicker!" Squid took a deep breath and walked over to a thin slice of shade next to a wall at the border of the lot. The one place that Squid would *not* go today would be the park, because that is where he would usually be hanging out. With Molly and Saw and Larry and who knows who else looking for him, he was an idiot to still be in the neighborhood. But the mission and the possibility of seeing Rachel kept him circling the area like an orbiting planet.

But what to do now? The afternoon still stretched ahead of him in its humid endlessness. He could see the clock in the tower easily from where he was. Two o'clock. Squid squatted down. There was nowhere to sit. He adjusted the little bat under his pants with a snort of irritation. Squid pulled out the three-by-five card Unc had given him. It said "Grandson" at the top. A poem was written on it: "In all your days prepare / And treat them ever alike. / When you are the anvil, bear, / When you are the hammer, strike."

Squid remembered a time that he and Unc were on the roof. They had taken some old wooden slats out of an empty room and placed them on the top of a battered metal trash can lid. Somehow Unc had gotten the wood to catch fire, and Squid had bought some hot dogs. There they were, roasting hot dogs on sticks, far above the shouting and honking below. Squid loved hot dogs.

"It feels good to be above things, doesn't it, Unc? I mean above all the heartache and suffering down below."

"Yes, grandson, it feels good. 'What is this world if full of care, we have no time to stand and stare . . .' This is what humans have been doing for thousands of generations, sitting around a fire, telling stories—"

"Feeling safe," Squid interrupted. "I like being here with you, Unc. I hate heights in one way, but in another way it gives me a good lookout point. I don't know why I get so jittery, Unc. I don't know why I am so nervous. You know I have real trust issues." Squid put another hot dog on his stick, hesitated, then thrust it into the fire. "I guess you are the closest thing to someone I can trust. You are someone I can depend on."

"Isn't it funny, Squid?" Unc stretched his legs out and looked up at the sky. "We bipeds spend so much time worrying and fretting, mostly about things that never happen. Once I was on the run and I had to hide in a cemetery in Brooklyn. I spent the whole afternoon there waiting for someone. I kept looking at the names on the stones. Some of them had died a hundred years ago. No one remembers one specific thing they were worried about. All the time they wasted being afraid, just think of that. Here, pass me that mustard, my dog is ready."

"I had some bad experiences, Unc, and I'm afraid they will happen again. Look." Squid lifted his shirt in the back a few inches, enough to show a crisscross of white scars on his skin. "You know I never saw a doctor as a kid? Not once. I was in a doctor's office once. Someone almost saw this. I thought they were going to help me. Then I got pulled away at the last minute. I screamed and held on like crazy. You should have seen me, Unc. Something in me didn't want to leave. I'll never, never forget that day. They could hardly pull me away from that office. But they did. And now I'm afraid bad things will happen again. That at the last moment, nobody will be there to protect me. I'm always thinking about it. You don't seem like you get scared, Unc. How do you do it?"

Unc was quiet for awhile. Then he sighed and lifted the bottle to his mouth. "Well, first I make sure I am never in situations where I will have to be brave. And then, grandson, I suppose that I remember that the coward dies a thousand deaths. Really bad things happen, but thinking about it all the time just destroys all the good times in between. Good times like this. You know, there's a region in Italy where they drink a glass of bitter wine before the meal because it makes the rest of the meal taste so much better in comparison. Tough times and fear are like bitter wine, Squid. They make this good time taste so much better. This squat is bitter wine. Living here makes these hot dogs taste like a feast for kings."

Unc put a potato chip in his mouth and chewed awhile. "Look at all those people on the streets down below us. They are about as big as cockroaches. They don't go on their roofs because there's a sign that says they are not supposed to and a siren goes off if they try to open the door. They never would build a fire that kisses the sky because a fire might damage the tar-and-felt covering on their precious roof. They feel sorry for you and me. But I'm not worried about damaging our roof, are you? I feel sorry for them. We are like gods up here, master of all we see, and they are like little mice hiding in their tiny, locked air-conditioned cubicles. They think they are rich, but they are gripped with fear. They are afraid for their property, afraid they can't pay the rent, afraid they'll lose their pension plan. They're afraid of everything."

Squid put another hot dog on his stick. "But how do you keep from feeling fear? I feel good right now, but it's only because I smoked some weed and I'm up here with you."

Unc fixed his eyes on Squid. "Sometimes you just have to act, Squid. Freedom can't be clutched with a trembling fist. Sometimes you just have to pull your sword out, like Alexander, and slice right through the Gordian knot. Acting decisively and waiting, acting decisively and waiting — it's the yin and yang of life."

Squid had turned the hot dog over so the other side would get brown just the way he liked it. "You must be in a waiting stage in your life right now, huh, Unc? I haven't seen you take too much decisive action. I don't know which Alexander you are talking about, but I get a knot in my stomach all the time. Do you think he could help me?"

Squid thought about Unc as he huddled under the little strip of shade in the lot. He couldn't remember anything else he said that night on the roof. He looked at the poem again. He got it. It was plain. He knew what an anvil was. He understood. He knew Unc was telling him to be a warrior. No longer was it time to bear. It was time to do the unexpected. He knew he would go to Saw's place and hit him in the neck or do something terrible. He wasn't going to run around all afternoon in terror. He felt as though he had a purpose again. He felt the way he felt at sunrise after putting away his envelope. He could walk right by Unc's begging spot on his way to his attack.

Squid walked and limped with purpose the few blocks to Unc's corner. Unc was sitting next to a chain-link fence under a tree of heaven that was growing out of the abandoned lot behind him. Jason, of all people, was squatting next to him. Unc's face was very red and he was overly happy to see Squid. "Grandson!" he shouted with a slight slur. "You're alive! Come over here and sit by me." Unc gestured dramatically. "You are just in time. Jason and I are having the most marvelous conversation." As Unc spoke, somebody walked by and dropped a few coins in Unc's cup. "Thank you, kind sir. God bless you, sir," Unc said without missing a beat. "You see, Jason doesn't realize that I am a parasite and that he has created me. He doesn't realize how defective I've really become because of his grand compassionate system."

"Hi, Squid. I'm sorry but I'm a little warmed up now." Jason turned back to Unc. "Look, I don't deny that you have a point. But what is your proposal? What is the alternative to compassion?"

"Well, certainly not this!" Unc spoke way too loud and gestured to the neighborhood around him. You and your 'religious' attitude have created this cesspool. Look at it! It's like the Bowery during the depression. You've provided the free food people can eat and even blankets and socks if they get cold. I'm especially glad about the blankets. Here they don't even have to scrape up a few coins for a flophouse. They stay in a cursed *squat* for free. Your church has created a wonderful environment for people like *me* to act like *this*. We can drink and shoot up and drive the last remaining decent businesses out of the area. Then the realtors will buy up all this property for nothing, for squat, if you'll pardon the expression, and develop it and make a million dollars on each studio apartment.

"In twenty years some snot-nosed kid with rich parents will be living in my squat that's been miraculously transformed into luxury apartments. He'll never even know what happened there. He'll pass by a drunk on the street and he'll never know I used to live where his swish living room is. He'll never know that someone like Squid here used to feed the birds out his window. He'll never know how you and your bleeding-heart church contributed to this sick alcoholic junkie culture. He'll never know how you helped some slick entrepreneur make a hundred million bucks off some poor Puerto Ricans and East Europeans who *used* to live here and who never knew what happened to their neighborhood, the neighborhood they grew up in."

Jason held up his hand. "Wait a minute, wait a minute. You are talking way too fast, and I'm not quite following the logic here." There was a hard edge to Jason's voice though he was trying to stay calm.

"The bottom line, the bottom line, Jason," Unc slurred, "is that you have forgotten, no, I don't think you ever knew, the iron rule. The iron rule is that you never do for someone else what they can do for themselves. Otherwise you create people like me."

"So what is the other choice? Should we throw you and Bonehead into work camps with a sign above them that says 'Work Makes Us Free'? Don't you think a dangerous thing happens when you begin to talk like you talk? Don't you think that the way you are talking opens the door for a kind of hardness and greed that is taking over the whole world? Think of those people just a few blocks away from here. They don't care. They are making millions on Wall Street. They can see the housing projects out their windows. But they don't want to know that none of the teenagers I've been assigned to work with can adequately read. These teenagers are smart. They can hustle like crazy. They are great businessmen on the streets. You know those people a few blocks away could help them *read*, for Pete's sake, help them do something besides get shot at thirty.

"But they don't want to see them. They want to listen to *you* so that they don't have to do anything. *You* give them an excuse not to think about it. That's what they really want. Then they can say it's not their problem. Now I'm not talking about bleeding-heart charity; I'm talking about fairness. Why do their children go to enriched programs and these children go to forlorn schools next to empty lots where they don't even learn how to read?"

"Ah, I notice you shifted gears," Unc interrupted with a dramatic wave of his hand. "I notice you began to talk about children rather than the sick addictive person like myself who is feeding off your good intentions, playing you like a fiddle. Who is the one who really refuses to see? Is it the stockbroker on Wall Street, Jason, or is it you?"

"Well, that is a good question. You've already pointed out that you can't do anything to help an alcoholic unless the alcoholic wants to change, haven't you? But really, how do you help someone to change?" Jason looked Unc right in the eye. "Is it not possible that real change might come through kindness? In the story of the prodigal son, didn't the father have to give his son everything and watch him walk down the road and learn the lesson for himself? Didn't the father in the story look like a sucker? Doesn't the alcoholic have to learn the lesson himself just like the prodigal son? Wasn't the son prodded by the kindness of a father who would never let go? Is that not, in the end, the only thing that will ever touch you?"

Unc took a drink and slouched his head over toward Jason. "What are you looking for here, Jason?" His words were venomous. "Are you looking for a story? Do you want to go home and tell your church how you told me about Jesus and got me saved? Really, Jason, is not your presence here one more selfish motive in your pampered and selfish life? Does it make you feel good to sort the silverware and clean the toilet for someone like me? As you can see, I am not grateful. Aren't you just some modern Jason, looking for adventure so you can go back and tell your little Argonauts about all that happened to you in that articulate, compassionate manner you have? I'm sure they will think you are a regular Mother Teresa. You are a talented young man. This little jaunt in the Lower East Side is just a phase for you. Tell you what. Let's meet again in twenty years. I will come and visit you in your beautiful home in the richest part of Connecticut, and we can reminisce together about the good old days here on the tough streets and the squats of the old Lower East Side."

Jason began to say something but stopped. He adjusted his weight on his haunches and looked across the street for awhile. Finally he stood up. "See you later, Squid." He walked back quickly in the direction of the mission.

Unc took another drink and finished off the bottle. "That went pretty well, I thought, didn't you, Squid?"

"What?"

"I think that with a few more little discussions, our young theologian will be convinced of the devilish influence of all churches in this neighborhood and the pernicious futility of his own pathetic work. How dare they come in with their bleeding hearts and provide food and help so that we can do what we want and drink and talk to our good friends all day!" Unc was talking very loud, and he patted Squid's hand as he said "good friends." "How despicable that he might use *me* as fodder for a story to tell at his college or his air-conditioned church with new cushions on its seats, while I sit here on a scrap of cardboard."

"Do you really think that, Unc?"

"No." Unc paused. "I am merely being his *provocateur*. I'm here to muddle him, to train him, like Socrates did."

"I don't know what you're talking about. No wonder Rachel likes him. I hate him." Squid looked up and down the street to make sure he didn't see Molly. He plowed ahead with his own thoughts. "But you know, Unc, what made me so mad? I tried to beg on First Avenue, and I got nothing. No one even looked at me. I felt like a piece of puke frying against the brick and the cement. No, worse than puke, because if I were a piece of puke, someone might have stopped and tried to clean it up. But I got nothing. I don't know what you're saying about the churches, but at least Jason wasn't afraid to squat down and looked me in the eye. At least he said my name. I wish it had been somebody else, anybody else . . ."

Unc wasn't listening. "But you are alive, my grandson, you are alive. The visitor at our squat when you made your timely exit was only Ratchet. He and Chaos were having a friendly disagreement when you left. But tell me your adventures and tell me especially about whether you made any money on First Avenue. This is such a big day for you. Everyone is asking about you. You've become quite the celebrity in the neighborhood."

"It's been nothing. I got two dollars from Jason but I spent it. I ran from Molly. I thought I had a job but I lost it. I almost killed Bonehead. But now I am going to really do something. I read your card. I'm going to take action. This is it. No more waffling for me."

Unc looked at Squid, still effusive. "Do you have any money left, my young warrior?"

Squid grimaced and pulled out the dollar bills from his back pocket. "I've got four dollars, Unc, but this might be the day I get killed. I might need some money for an emergency."

"There, there," Unc said. "Remember, think like a warrior. I tell you what." Unc leaned his face very close to Squid's. "If you hand me those dollar bills, I promise I will stand guard over you tonight so that you can get some beauty rest for your time with Rachel and Jason. I'll be there to protect you. Who knows? Rachel might be the Beatrice to your Dante. She might lead you to the celestial rose. I pass you off into her care as you pass from the inferno and purgatory into paradise."

"You really will be there and stand guard over me tonight? Would you do that, Unc? And who is this Beatrice? Is she a friend of Rachel's?"

Unc smiled a boozy smile. "Between the money in your hand and my summer thirst lies my promise, my grandson." Unc reached out his hand.

"OK." Squid handed over the crumpled bills. "But tell me this, Unc. About that card you have on your wall that talks about angels. You said you don't believe that. You said it's not true, but it's beautiful. I can't get that out of my head. Like, how can something be really, really beautiful, if it is not really, really true?"

Unc's eyes grew wide in mock astonishment. "Squid, you always surprise me. You are not really a warrior. You are a Greek philosopher." Unc leaned over again close to Squid. "I'll tell you a secret. I'll tell you what I really, really believe. It's deeper than beauty or truth. I'll tell you what the true, true foundation of my faith is. Here it is— randomness." Unc slapped his hands on his knees and leaned back. "That's it. Randomness. Rock-solid, dependable randomness. I worship at the altar of randomness. That is the true foundation. That is the turtle upon which the whole world, the whole universe is resting. And you know what else I think, Squid? Have you ever seen those little Ping-Pong balls with numbers on TV that fly up and tell you if you won the lottery?"

"No, I haven't watched TV for a long time."

"Well, you have to see this. It's a tribute to total, pure chance, and they interrupt the evening news to tell you this. I've watched it on the TV in the bars. There's all these little Ping-Pong balls bouncing around in total chaos, and a few fly up this air shaft and tell you if you have won. A beautiful woman stands beside them and reads the numbers aloud. Well, Squid, in terms of my life, the Ping-Pong balls with my numbers never flew up. And neither did yours. That is why I am here, sitting on a piece of cardboard. However, it is still amusing to sit here and watch the show."

"So, everything that happens to us is just a jumble of Ping-Pong balls."

"That's it. Now I will tell you what interests me. There's no reason or purpose for it to interest me; it just does. Courage in the face of randomness. The soul wanders through this random suffering and joy, mostly suffering, and some bear it like an anvil and strike like a hammer. That is where you come in." Unc looked at Squid with a knowing smile. "Now, warrior, I think you have something to do. Whatever it is, go for it, my grandson."

"Right. See you at the squat." Squid got up and started walking and limping toward Saw's place.

CHAPTER 8

SAW'S PLACE WAS only a few blocks away. Squid turned the corner and scanned the street for evil-wishers. Down the street, resting on a rolled up mattress, was a man with long blond hair, relaxing in the shade. His feet stretched out on the sidewalk so that people had to step over his boots. It was Ratchet. He had his hands folded behind his head like a cowboy. Squid came up next to him and sat down by him. Ratchet opened his eyes and closed them again. His pet python, Snappy, was coiled next to him and didn't move.

"You are swimming in some kind of shark pit today, aren't you, Squid?"

Squid straightened his knee out so the bat under his pants didn't hurt him. He nodded and then realized that Ratchet's eyes were closed. "Yep," he said. Ratchet smiled with his eyes closed and Squid laughed. "I don't know which way is up, Ratchet."

"You got that right."

"Ratchet, if I, um, get the hundred bucks I owe Saw, will you give it to him? I mean, I just need someone who can pass it on to him, you know."

"Nope, I won't." Ratchet stretched his legs out a little further. "Things are getting pretty deep, now, Squid. You're in a really deep pit, man. I don't think you understand. The longer you avoid him, the madder he gets."

"It's not like you think, Ratchet. Saw is ruining my rep. He's destroying my name, and it's not all true. Couldn't you help me, Ratchet?"

Ratchet kept his eyes closed. "Nope. Me and Snappy here are keeping our options open. Big stuff is coming down, Squid. Big stuff. We're getting a whole system now. Where squatters pay rent to us, and if they don't, they're in trouble. It's a great business. Who are the squatters going to call, the police? They'd find their illegal rears on the streets faster than you could say nine-one-one. You could be a part of this if you wanted, Squid, if you got your heart right. There's some good money in it, and it's not too hard."

Squid rolled up his shirt in his hands as tight as he could. "You mean, like beating people up if they don't give you money? Like going into a squat like mine and cracking heads unless they cough up some money? Is that what you are talking about?"

"It's just collecting rent, that's all, and when you work together, there aren't so many problems. All you got to do is scare a few people, and then the system works OK. Just make sure you're not one of the people they have to scare, Squid."

"Who is this 'they' you are talking about, Ratchet? You are freaking me out again, man. Seriously."

Ratchet crossed one of his cowboy boots over the other. "It's like a whole system. But the people in this system keep their word. That's what it's all about. Just scare a few people. Scare 'em by doing what you say you're going to do. Then everybody else just falls in line. There's still a chance for you, Squid. You're either for him or against him. You know what I mean. But if you don't make up your mind pretty soon and join 'em, you could get yourself skinned alive, man."

"What are you talking about, Ratchet?"

"You know you're being watched, doncha? Just be careful who you hang out with. It's been noticed that you hang around the mission a lot. I'd hate to see one of those nice people get hurt just because of you."

"What are you talking about? Ratchet, you are freaking me out." Squid stood up. "You're like somebody I don't know, man. You're somebody I thought I could trust. Well, man, I got other things I got to do today. Don't tell anyone you saw me, OK? See ya."

Ratchet just nodded a good-bye and kept his eyes closed. Snappy didn't move.

Squid kept heading toward Saw's place. It wasn't really Saw's place, of course. It was Molly's. Molly had been in that place forever. It seemed to Squid that Saw had brutalized Molly there forever. He treated her like a slave. Molly was a junkie. Sometimes Squid had seen her standing on the street outside her tenement building with her eyes closed. Her whole body would be listing to one side. Every now and then she would jerk upwards a bit, as if she were waking up. She would straighten up slightly, then in a doze, she would begin listing again to the side. Squid never knew how long she would do that. He would always just walk by.

Molly would do whatever she needed to do to get some money. She was not attractive. She looked like an old woman. She was a prostitute for a handful of dollars. Her face looked like an old punching bag. Squid didn't know if Saw was the one who broke her nose so bad. Maybe it had been broken a bunch of times.

Saw didn't beat her privately. He did it on the street. "Shut up!" he would shout at her and backhand her across the face. She would whimper and follow behind him. "Hurry up!" he'd shout even louder and push her to the ground. Molly would get up obediently and pick up her things. If Saw would let her, she would follow him everywhere, looking down and not speaking, like a whipped dog.

Once Squid saw them snuggling together in the park. Saw had his arm around her protectively and held a cup of coffee in the other hand. She sat next to him with her head resting on his shoulder, a cup of coffee in one hand and a long-stem rose in the other. Her broken bag face had a dreamy smile on it. For a moment as Squid walked across the park, he felt a twinge of pity for the couple. Here was Saw, powerful and still young, taking care of this beat-up shell of a person. She looked more like his ailing mother than his lover or whatever she was to him.

Yet the next time he saw them together, Saw came up behind her and kicked her so hard that her feet lifted off the ground. Molly landed on her feet, stumbled a bit, and slunk down the street like a beaten cur with a bad owner.

How Molly kept from being evicted, Squid could only guess. Her tenement building was very old. The building itself looked like a bag lady with sheets and trash hanging out of some windows and everything looking frumpy and greasy. Squid had never been inside her apartment but knew they lived on the second floor in the back. This knowledge gave him a chance to see if the fire escape would give him any possibility of access. Squid had been behind the building before, and the visibility from any of the reputable buildings was limited enough that he could snoop around if he didn't waste much time.

Squid did not know what he was going to do. He didn't know what Unc thought he was going to do. But Squid felt like a general, somehow, who was striking at the heart of his enemy's headquarters. His opponents had really spread themselves too thin, ranging far and wide looking for him. They had gotten too cocky.

Squid circled through a vacant lot and got to the back of the building. He had to pick his way through a lot of broken glass and metal, but he had become so accustomed to favoring his right foot that he didn't even think about it. It was a relief for him to feel focused and purposeful again. If Saw were there, Squid would kill him. He felt like a scout, looking for whatever opportunities for damage that might arise. He had no plan; he just wanted to strike like a hammer and see what happened.

Sure enough, there was the fire-escape ladder, hanging ten feet above the ground. Squid found some old milk crates and put them on top of each other. Squid checked again to see if anyone was looking out a window anywhere in the area. He quickly scrambled on the milk crates and reached the bottom rung of the fire-escape ladder. He pulled himself up and twisted like a monkey to get a foothold. The bat inside his pants hit the ladder, making a lot more noise than he had hoped to. The ladder rattled as he scrambled up. He stayed still for a moment to see if anyone looked out Molly's windows. There was no need now to look around suspiciously at the other windows. He just needed to do what he needed to do as quickly as possible.

Squid climbed up very quietly, pretending he was a ninja. When he reached the platform of the second floor, he moved as smoothly as a cat. He squatted against the wall next to the window that faced the fire-escape platform. So far so good. No one had looked out the window, and he had heard no movements.

A very old collapsible gate stretched across the main window. Squid faced the wall and put his hand on the edge of the window. Slowly he edged his face toward the window so that he could see who was inside. He could hear nothing. Maybe they were asleep. That would be a good opportunity. He inched half of his face across the edge so that he could see.

No one was in the room. In the center was an old, rickety table with about fifty different candles on it and some hypodermic needles. None of the candles was lit. The walls were dark and covered with something, but the windows were too dirty for Squid to see what it was. He edged his head further over so that he could see more. A brown-crusted stove and some ancient cabinets were in one corner, but he could see no more.

Now to get in. He lifted the sash of the window. It screeched opened. Squid froze for a moment but knew that he couldn't stay out in full view on the fire escape forever in the middle of the day. Perhaps the grate would open also. Squid had space enough to reach a hand inside. He grabbed the bottom of the grate to see if it would slide over. It wouldn't give.

Squid reached his hand in further to see if he could feel where the grating met the edge of the window. Squid knew that these metal gratings should be designed to open from the inside in case of fire, but this was not one of those. He felt the padlock and it was locked tight. Could he slide through at the top or at the bottom? No way.

For a moment, Squid had a vision of setting fire to the apartment, and seeing Saw clutching at the padlocked grate, gulping in black smoke, but Squid had seen too many squats burn. You never knew where the fire would go or who might get hurt. People were probably smart enough to get out, but he hated thinking about some little dog or cat getting stuck somewhere, not knowing how to get out.

Squid looked inside the window again. No sign of anyone there. He noticed an open door leading to another room next to the room he had looked into. On the outside wall, he looked over to the back window from that adjacent room. The window was wide open. No grating, not even a screen. Why hadn't he noticed that when he was climbing up? Of course, it could safely be left wide open because the fire escape did not run close enough to it.

Still, Squid thought there might be some possibilities. If he could stand on the railing of the fire escape with his left foot, he might be able to reach the top of the window with his right hand and reach the bottom of the window ledge with his sore right foot. It was risky, but since the window was wide open, he might be able to cling to the wall for the moment he needed to step over, and then get his feet on the ledge and his hand under the top of the window. Then he could just pop right in.

Squid did not know if anyone was in the room. He would need both hands to try the feat, and he would not be able to hold his bat out to defend himself. He tried not to think about what it would feel like to have Saw's big knife thrust in his gut as he clutched the outer window. He couldn't help but wonder about the sound of his back hitting the broken glass below. He'd heard that thud before when some junkie fell out the second-floor window at his squat. It was louder than he'd thought it would be.

Squid still could hear no movement inside the apartment. He climbed on the metal railing and stood balanced there on his left foot. He still didn't like heights. He grabbed the top of the window opening with his right hand. He stepped on the window ledge with his sore foot. His foot was tender, but if he placed it right, it didn't hurt too badly. For a brief moment, before he could hook his arm under the top of the open window, he would be suspended with no sure way to hold on. But it would be just a moment. He pushed himself toward the window and hooked his arm under the open windowpane. No problem. In another minute, with a little wrangling, he got himself inside the window and plopped on the floor. *Just like Superman,* he thought.

The room was empty. Squid stood there motionless. The smell of soiled clothes and heat filled his senses. Total silence. He held his breath and listened for breathing. As he stood there longer, he could hear one horsefly buzzing in the next room. Since the room faced the back, he could hear only the sound of a solitary air conditioner far away and some distant traffic noise.

Someone could be in the other room, asleep or waiting for him. Squid continued motionless and listening. He couldn't figure it out. There must be someone in the other room. Even though he couldn't hear anything, he sensed a presence. It didn't feel like an empty apartment. It felt like an apartment with some evil person or thing in it. Squid had jumped through a lot of windows and been in a lot of abandoned buildings where terrible things were happening, but he had never felt something like this. Probably it was just because he knew it was Saw's apartment. Saw scared Squid and made him stutter even when he saw him on the street, and here he was breaking into Saw's apartment. Maybe Saw was waiting for him in the other room just like he was waiting for Saw in this room.

"Into the mouth of the wolf," Unc would say. The room was small with only a mattress on the floor. Dirty clothes were scattered everywhere. A broken chair lay on its side in one of the corners. One of the legs looked loose. Squid moved very slowly, stepping on the sides of his feet toward the chair. He carefully reached out and grabbed the loose leg of the chair and pulled. It wouldn't give. Shifting his weight to get some leverage, he twisted the leg. The sound of old glue cracking seemed louder than a pistol shot to Squid. The leg came loose and Squid stood still a long time. It was only then that he remembered that he had his stupid little bat dangling from his leg.

Stepping on the sides of his feet and rolling them inward, Squid laboriously made his way to the door to the other room. The floor creaked a little bit but not much. It took him a long time to make it across the room. As he got closer, the room still looked empty. There the candles were on the table, the needles, and some other small objects. Squid tried to imagine Saw standing next to the door, huge knife in hand, waiting for Squid to stick his idiotic head in. Surely the apartment was empty, but Squid hesitated because the other room seemed to have an atmosphere, a force field all its own. The sound of the horsefly got louder and louder as he got closer to the room.

Squid crept to the edge of the door to get the best angle on the place of possible ambush. Nothing. He poked his head completely in the door to get a full view. Nothing. Unless someone was in the bathroom, the place was empty. Why was Squid's heart still pounding so hard? He raised the leg of the chair above his shoulder and walked quickly toward the bathroom. The bathroom was dirty and tiny and empty except for clothes dangling from a bar.

Squid didn't know if someone had watched him climb in the window. He didn't know when Saw or Molly or whoever else lived there would come back. He walked over to the door. It had two dead bolts and a third lock underneath the doorknob. Both the dead bolts were locked, but the one beneath the doorknob was not. Good. He flipped the lever to lock it. Someone would have to unlock three locks to get at him. He tried to flip on the light, but the lights didn't work.

Squid couldn't get over the sense of otherness he felt. His skin tingled even though it was very hot. Whatever the presence was, it was dark and threatening. Squid paused for a moment. Someone was coming up the stairs. The footsteps were very loud as they reached the second floor. They walked toward Saw's apartment and stopped for a moment. Then they kept climbing to the next floor.

He sensed bad vibes even more strongly as he walked over to the table with the array of candles on it. Along with the hypodermic needles, a bunch of little metal and pewter figurines were scattered about. He picked up one. It was a skull. Another was a little hand giving the finger. Another was a pentagram. There was a small figure of a curved dagger. There was a metal swastika. These things were fairly common in the neighborhood, especially where people were shooting up. Why did he feel so funny? In his gut he knew he was in way over his head, and he could not take on Saw or whatever else was in this room. Maybe he was getting sick. Why did he actually feel cold even though the room was horribly humid?

Squid's eyes became more accustomed to the dimness. This room stunk more than the other room. Squid turned around to see what the horsefly was buzzing around. Along the side wall was a narrow, crude work table. On top of the table was a pine board with something nailed to it, and that something was what the fly was attracted to. Squid took a step forward and looked more closely. This was the source of the smell.

It was a freshly killed squirrel. It had been crudely skinned with its paws, its tail, its ears, and its belly nailed to the board. Freshly dried blood was still smeared on the board. Squid looked up in disgust and noticed that older skins had been nailed to the wall. He saw the skins of a Chihuahua, a poodle, a German shepherd. The skins of a gray cat, a black cat, and a calico cat intertwined with the skins of the dogs to make a vast jigsaw puzzle out of dead fur along the wall.

Squid felt a little sick to his stomach. He tried to remember what he was doing there. He put his hands in his pockets and felt the red crayon he'd picked up earlier in the day. It was only a few hours ago, but it seemed like centuries from where he was now. He took the crayon out and went over to the pine board that the squirrel was nailed to. He couldn't think of anything dangerous or clever to say. He put his crayon to an open space on the board and pressed down hard. He printed in block letters one word. He went over the letters repeatedly so that they would stand out bold and red. Finally he stepped back and studied his work. You could see it clearly even in the dark. WRONG. If only Unc had been there, Squid thought, he could have helped Squid write some smart quote or something. He put the crayon back in his pocket.

Squid truly wished he could have thought of something better to say, but that was the only thing he could come up with. He heard someone else, someone big coming up the stairs. The steps reached the second floor. Squid clutched the leg of the chair that he had ready as a weapon. This was it. This was the reason Squid had come here. Sure Saw had a knife, but Squid had the element of surprise. He would swing at his ugly face and crack his sunglasses and put an end to the wrong things this man did to animals and people like Squid. Just a few moments of strength, and Squid would not be afraid anymore. He just had to remember to swing up because Saw was so much bigger than he was.

Squid could hear the steps walking down the hallway toward the door that Squid was standing against. Heavy steps. Like someone wearing boots. This was it. The moment of truth. Squid heard the keys tinkle as someone fumbled with them on the other side of the door. There was still time.

Like lightning, Squid dashed into the other room and headed for the window, tossing the chair leg on some dirty clothes. As he crouched on the ledge of the window, he heard the noise of the first dead bolt being unlocked. Squid jumped for the railing of the fire escape and caught with each hand a vertical bar. His legs flailed in the air while he worked to swing his arm to catch the ladder's edge below the second-floor platform. He caught the ladder and shot down to the last rung. He dangled his legs down until he felt the milk crates and let go. The milk crates did not collapse, and he was able to jump off in a flash. He hit the ground running and limping as fast as he could.

Squid ran along the back of some buildings and picked his way through some rolls of old chain-link fence. Squid's mind felt like Unc's jumble of Ping-Pong balls. He could turn left and make a break for it on the street. But Saw's building faced that street. Perhaps Saw was thinking the same thing and had already run to the street to intercept Squid. If Saw had any "friends" around, he could station one at each of the two diagonal corners of the block as lookouts. They could catch Squid no matter where he left the block.

Squid turned right and snaked his way behind the buildings of the block. An old board fence blocked his way completely, but he found a missing board and continued his retreat. Maybe Saw hadn't even heard him leave. Maybe it wasn't Saw. Maybe Saw didn't have a key to the bottom lock. Maybe Saw was quietly searching behind the buildings right now. It would be an ideal place to trap Squid. Saw could do anything he wanted and no one would see him. Squid saw a quick image of Saw skinning that pet German shepherd but forced it out of his mind.

Squid continued picking his way behind the buildings. There was no alley, but many of the buildings didn't go back to the property line, so there was a little bit of space behind them. Squid finally came to a reedy vacant lot, twenty feet wide, with lots of brick and broken glass and garbage in it. This lot led to the street on the opposite side of the block from Saw's street. The remains of an old refrigerator box were propped up next to some chairs. The old chain-link fence on the front of the lot had been rolled back so that anyone could walk in.

Squid did not want to go on the street yet. His shirt was half-soaked in sweat. He pulled up an old milk crate and positioned it behind the refrigerator box. Here he could sit for a moment and no one could see him from the street. It was the best place he could find to let things calm down a bit.

Squid sat on the crate and rested his head against the old brick wall. He couldn't quite understand why Saw's apartment had upset him so much. He just felt that he was in way over his head, that he was condemned, that he was a target for something vastly more powerful and evil than he was, and that it was only a matter of time. Squid felt sick to his stomach. He closed his eyes and breathed deeply. At least he was in the shade. The day was very warm.

Squid wanted to be in a place that was air-conditioned. He remembered being in his own room when he was fifteen years old. Sure, they moved around a lot and they always rented, but this was the nicest room he had ever had. It was summer and the window air conditioner in his room was huge. His room felt like a refrigerator, and it was great. He had his headphones on, and he was listening to some sports announcer on the radio giving the baseball scores for the day. Every time the announcer would say the word *Yankees*, he would touch his Yankees pennant three times and say, "One, two, three." Maybe he was the happiest he'd ever been. He had his own room. No one was bothering him. He had no friends at the new school, but he didn't care. His mom was messed up and she saw lots of men, but she had always been like that. The announcer said the name *Reggie Jackson* and the word *Yankees* in the same sentence, so he touched the pennant nine times just for emphasis.

A feeling swept over him, like colors and music and a home run all at the same time. "This must be what it feels like to be happy," he said out loud, even though he couldn't hear himself because of the headphones. He opened his dresser drawer, reaching to the back of it and gently pulling out his envelope with the red border and green writing. He wanted to do something, but he didn't know what to do. He was thankful, but he didn't know who to thank. His mom? No. The air conditioner? No. The Yankees? No.

He took off the headphones. The announcer was talking about the Red Sox anyway. He got out a clean sheet of paper and looked for a pen, but all he could find was a Magic Marker. Life felt so big and strange and good, he wanted to say thank you to somebody. He poised the Magic Marker in his hand above the paper for a long time. The paper felt so clean and fresh to his fingertips. Finally he wrote "THIS IS GREAT" as neatly as he could across the page. He carefully folded the paper, taking his time and matching the edges of the paper exactly together. He stopped for a moment, getting ready to put this new sheet of paper into the envelope. He slowly tapped one-two-three around the red border. He just sat there, listening to the air conditioner. For once he didn't have to bite his thumbs. His stomach didn't hurt at all.

There was a knock at the door and his mom came in. She had a bright red scarf around her neck and had just had her hair done. Her face was flushed with excitement, and her eyes were so wide he could see the whites all the way around her irises.

"I have some good news to tell you, son. At least I think it's good news. I mean, it's good news for me. I mean, I think you are going to understand it, once you, like, understand it. I mean, I think you're going to be glad because it makes me glad." His mom sat down on the bed and put her hands in her lap. "You know I have been pretty lonely lately, and the one man who really meant something to me has come back in my life. Now, don't bite your thumbs like that, you know how that hurts my heart when you do that. Anyway, Sammy is going to be coming over here this afternoon for the first time in a long, long time, and I just want you to be nice to him. I know that we had some strange times in the past, and I know that you feel that I didn't protect you and that I didn't tell the truth with the caseworker and the police and all that. I know that you and I never saw the doctor, but this is really important to me now, and you've just got to help me.

"You're my son and you're the most important thing in the world to me, but I am very lonely and he has really changed. I know he has, sweetie. Besides, now you are bigger, and you are the man of the house, and you can protect yourself. It won't be like it was, honest, and we will be one happy family because he is really the man I've always loved. Sometimes in life, you just have to face things, even if they are hard, and do the best you can. You have to be brave. That's what this is all about. Don't ruin your shirt like that, you'll get it all wrinkled. In fact . . . I didn't really tell you the truth, sweetie, because he is in the living room right now, and I want you to come out and see him. Now be nice, please, honey."

His mom reached out to touch his shoulder, and he pulled back. "Sure, Mom," he said very quietly. "Just give me a minute. I'll be out there in a minute. I'm bigger now. I can protect you."

"Great!" she said and floated to the door. "I'll see you in a minute."

After the door was closed, Squid stood up and put all the money from his drawer into his pocket. He folded his envelope and deliberately put it in his other pocket. He took the clean white folded piece of paper and crumpled it up into a wad and then even tighter. He slammed the paper into the wastebasket and walked out the door of his room. In the hallway, he turned toward the living room and listened to the voices. He could hear his mom laughing like the sounds of tinkling bells.

He stood there and twisted his hands up into his shirt until the neckline stretched so tight he thought it might snap. Then he turned away from the living room and quietly opened the back door. He walked out into their backyard. The heat almost felt good. He could still hear the sound of his huge air conditioner. He jumped over the back fence, crossed another yard, and found himself on the road headed toward the bus station. That was the last time he ever saw his mom.

Squid had lost track of time as he sat on the crate next to the abandoned building. Now he was older. He thought again about how cool that air-conditioning was in his room. He was just about to drift into a light sleep as he sat on the crate. His eyes were still closed, but he heard the soft crunching of gravel right next to him. Squid opened his eyes. There was Cheese with red hair and bulging eyes and a short section of pipe raised above his head, ready to strike.

CHAPTER 9

SQUID ROLLED TOWARD the ground as the pipe crashed toward where his head was. As it struck the wall behind him, the pipe made a huge noise and sliced off a sliver of old brick. As Squid rolled, he felt something else hit him in the back. It was Squeaky, Cheese's motherly girlfriend. She had an old tire iron. She scored a fairly square shot as Squid rolled.

Squid got to his feet in a flash and felt for his bat. The three squared off for a brief moment and looked at each other. In the hot afternoon, everything was clear. No one was watching. Cheese and Squeaky were amateurs. Cheese was the stronger and more dangerous, but if Squid went after him, Squeaky would whack him with that tire iron.

Squeaky was the one between Squid and the street. Squid bolted past Squeaky. Squeaky swung with the iron but it only hit a glancing shot on Squid. Squid ignored the pain in his foot but knew that he couldn't run very far. People. He needed to be around other people, and he would be safe.

Squid stepped through the fence and onto the sidewalk. Cheese and Squeaky were right behind him. No one was on the sidewalk. Only a car was cruising up the block. Squid jumped in front of it, holding his hands out. The car hit the brakes and stopped with a screech just as it touched Squid's hands.

Squid was not hurt, but he rolled on the ground and curled up in a fetal position. A big man, spitting out Spanish, got out of the car and marched to where Squid was curled up on the street. Several people opened their windows. A few people joined the driver as he stood over Squid. Cheese and Squeaky held onto their weapons but drifted back into the vacant lot and stood and watched.

Squid kept his eyes closed and counted to three nine times. Then he tried to think like a warrior. Was Saw around? Was Saw standing over him? Had Cheese or Squeaky, eager for twenty bucks, run to tell Saw?

Squid didn't move and he didn't open his eyes. Everyone was standing over him and talking. "What the heck is wrong with you, kid? Did you see what happened? Call an ambulance. He's just a homeless guy, but he's crazy."

The ambulance came faster than Squid expected. He kept his eyes shut, but he heard the sirens and could feel the heat of its engine as it parked next to him. Everyone tried to explain what happened. "This homeless guy just jumped in front of the car, and he hasn't moved since." Squid could imagine how bored the paramedics looked. They always looked that way when they came to the park.

"What's your name?" One of the medics was squatting next to him and speaking very loudly. "Hey, what's your name?" Squid was making a plan. Unc would be so proud.

"Squid," he finally said but kept his eyes closed.

"OK, Squid, but what's your real name? We have to know."

The little crowd of people that had gathered around was now quiet. Squid finally answered. "I don't remember. I think I hit my head when I hit the ground."

The medics fussed over him and talked him into uncurling from the fetal position. They got the stretcher out. "We're going to have to take you to the hospital, Squid, and check you out."

"OK," Squid said feebly. The police arrived. The medics got him into the ambulance. He was strapped on a stretcher. Only when he was inside did he open his eyes. Squid watched how the medic shut the door and locked it. *Easy*, he thought. The ambulance moved and the sirens went on. The ambulance turned and they drove about six blocks. Even though the sirens were on, the ambulance had slowed down to a standstill, probably trying to get through traffic on First Avenue. Squid thought about just staying in the ambulance, maybe even talking to a doctor. But what if the doctor made him stay in the hospital overnight or something? Squid thought about Rachel. Then he quietly undid the restraining belts that were on him in the ambulance.

The driver was talking on the radio, and the other medic was leaning forward to talk to him. "Do the Yankees play tomorrow?" the medic asked the driver. While the two were talking, Squid jumped up from the stretcher and unlocked the back door. He pushed down on the door handle and pushed out on the door. In the same motion, he jumped out and ran down the street. The medics didn't even try to chase him.

Squid turned the corner and slowed down. He thought Unc would be proud of him, and he wanted to tell him what he had done. Maybe everyone would think he was in the hospital for a little while. But he had to get off the street. Where could he go? Not to his squat. He should go find Unc. Now his stomach still felt like that jumble of Ping-Pong balls that Unc talked about. Something held him back. Sure, he could tell Unc about breaking into Saw's apartment and getting away from Cheese and Squeaky. Squid stopped walking on the street.

What was bugging Squid so much? It was still the strange presence Squid felt in Saw's apartment. It was that fly and the squirrel and the candles. Squid felt as though he was dealing with something far beyond anything he could handle or understand.

"I'll just go by the mission on my way to Unc," Squid muttered and walked down Avenue B. He saw a poster sign on the storefront chapel. "Memorial Service for Peaches— 3 p.m. today."

Squid walked over to the corner to see the clock on the Con Ed building. It was ten after three. Squid looked both ways on the street, quietly opened the storefront door, and stepped very carefully into the room.

Squid had known Peaches. Most of the time she was drunk and shouting in the park. She fought everyone. One time he saw her take off her shirt and fight a man. She was wearing an old bra and her muscles stuck out like ropes as she hit the man's face. When Squid had heard that she was dead, he had talked to Unc up on the roof.

"Do you think anyone will ever remember us here, Unc?"

Unc was packing a pipe as he sat upon the roof. He had an old cherrywood pipe that he only smoked if someone gave him some tobacco. Squid figured Unc didn't care whether he smoked or not. Unc didn't care about most things, except having a bottle hidden in his blanket. He took his time in answering Squid's question. "No, Squid, no one will remember us here. We think everything we do is so important. But it is only a survival skill humans acquired long ago so that we could keep on living without despair. All this will pass away. No one will remember this tobacco, this Chinese food that we find so delectable tonight." Unc stretched his legs out and wrapped the sheet around him as happy as a king. "Flowers think their bloom lasts forever, you know. We humans see it as a brief blush of color and then it's gone. That is what life is like, if someone else looked at our little dash of flesh and consciousness."

Unc found a match finally and took his time lighting his pipe. "It's all like smoke, really. We delude ourselves, Squid, into thinking any of this matters. It's all a matter of perspective. It's all a matter of time. Look at that length of rope over there, Squid. Probably the landlord did something with that a few years ago. Maybe they used it on that pulley over there to unload trash. That rope is still strong. If you look at it for what it can do in the next ten minutes, it is very strong. If I made a noose and hanged myself with that rope, it would kill me. I would feel the bristles dig into my neck as the weight of my body broke my neck or I was slowly asphyxiated."

"Stop it, Unc. You know I hate it when you talk like that."

"But, you know, Squid, if I look at that rope through the spectacles of thirty years, it's a very transitory thing. In a few years it will rot and be as frail as ashes, like a burnt fuse. It will have no more substantiality than a gossamer wing."

"What in the world are you talking about, Unc?"

"Or look at this neighborhood, grandson. Right now all these squats seems so real and so important. So permanent and substantial. But if you look through the perspective of a hundred years, this neighborhood has gone through more colors than a flower garden—Germans, Italians, Jews, Eastern Europeans, Puerto Ricans, now squatters. It will not last long. It will change hues faster than the leaves of fall. No, Squid, our life is like a smoke ring, like this smoke ring . . . aaah. See, it lasts for just a moment."

"Yeah, but Unc, it doesn't feel like smoke. It feels like it matters. I mean, like, good times. Like now, eating this food, looking out over the neighborhood. It feels great. It's better than a home run." Squid took a spring roll from the bag and gnawed on it. "It feels like, like you and me talking here, like it matters, like something here is going to last."

"Do you really want the rats here to last? Do you want this pathetic broken down squat to stay here? Do you want the roaches, the filth, the needles, the sewage here to last?" Unc blew a smoke ring.

"But what about the good things, Unc? What about you and me talking here and nobody bothering us and feeling free and nobody telling us what to do? That's like, something great, that's like something they should make a statue about. Like, someone should make a statue of you and me lying out on this roof. No, I don't mean that." Squid bit his thumb hard and started again. "Like, it feels better than that, Unc. Like this matters more than stone. Like, even if we died and nobody remembered anything about us, like, it would still be here and it would matter."

Unc looked at Squid and took another draw on his pipe. The sky was getting darker, and several points of music could be heard in the distance from open windows. Unc laughed and found a nail with a wide head and patted down the top of his tobacco. "Well, Squid, it does feel like it matters sometimes, but I don't think anyone is going to carve a statue to us or even remember our names."

Squid wouldn't let go of it. "Like, when you die, Unc. Do you think that's it? What about someone you love but haven't seen but remember all the good things they did? What if you don't know if she's dead or not? What if she took care of you as a kid and you never saw her for a long time? If she dies, is that it? Do they just put her in a coffin if she's lucky and then her face turns all brown and dried? Don't you think something more happens if the one person who ever loved you died? Isn't there something else that should happen to make things right?"

Unc stood up. "You can see one star over there, Squid. It's the evening star. 'I know enough of life and love to know that life is not the end of things.' A great poet once said something like that. But I don't believe it, Squid. I've seen some of my compadres die here in the squats before. Most of the time they drank themselves to death. But when I found them stiff and dead and as cold as meat in a freezer, I think simply that that's all there is. I look at their ashen face and all I see is an ashen face. You touch their hands when they're dead, and the hands feel like some little sticks in a skin bag. That's what I remember. It would be nice to think that there is something more, but that is just an illusion."

Squid got up close to Unc and wrapped his arms around his own knees really tight. "What's it like to touch a dead person, Unc? Does it make you sad? Does it make you want to make things right? Does it make you think that maybe there's something more out there than just eating Chinese food?"

"It makes me thirsty," Unc said. "Is there anything else to drink? Why don't you go get me something, Squid."

Squid shook his head to remember where he was as he entered the mission chapel. The carpeted floor gave a little and squawked like a disturbed pigeon. About ten people were sitting randomly around on the few rows of wooden pews. The pews were scarred and gnarled and looked like old, toothless boxers sprawled across the mat. The people in the pews were singing a dreary hymn, and many of them stopped singing to turn around and look at Squid. The song leader was another kitchen worker at the dining room, and he floundered bravely to finish the song. As he finished, hot silence reigned except for the regular rattle of another old ceiling fan.

Rachel was sitting alone on the front row, staring at the song leader. Squid could see only the outline of her cheekbone and her short brown hair above the back of the pew. He sat down on the back pew, but his stomach felt as though he'd sat on a park seesaw. For a few precious moments, he could watch her without anyone watching him. He felt guilty, as if he were doing something wrong, as if he were looking at some of the pornography that Unc had at the squat. No, it wasn't like pornography. Squid only had the highest thoughts for Rachel. He was just afraid someone was going to catch him watching her.

Slowly the kitchen worker pulled a piece of paper out of his pocket and said, "As you know, Peaches disappeared a few weeks ago and no one knew what happened to her. We didn't even know how to contact anybody, because everybody knows her as Peaches. We didn't know who her family was. We didn't even know a last name so that we could check the hospitals. We really didn't know her real first name, either."

"She has a sister in California! She told me about it once!" The sweating man on the second row looked like he wanted to say more, as if he were cranking up for the kind of speech that gushes out and never stops.

Several people said, "Shh!"

The kitchen worker fumbled with his paper and gripped it as if it were the last life jacket on a sinking ship. "Yeah, right. Anyway, you can talk to me after the service if you have any more information. As you know, the police have found a body in a squat that they think might be her. But they don't know for sure. The body was pretty cut up and part of the skin was removed." The people in the pews groaned.

"It can't be her!" the sweating man shouted. "She would never let anyone do something like that to her. She was too much of a fighter. If they did it to her, there must have been twenty of them. She's too tough!"

"Shut up!" someone in the back of the room shouted.

"No, you shut up," came the brilliant reply.

"OK, OK," the kitchen worker said and took a deep breath as if he were trying to keep from gulping in gallons of water. "So anyway, the police still don't have any other name for Peaches, and they're doing the best they can. We figured we ought to have a memorial service, as we sometimes do, because we figure this may be the only funeral Peaches gets." The kitchen worker straightened out his crumpled paper and began to read. "Peaches was in the park for many years and everybody knows her. She drank a lot, and she fought a lot—"

"One afternoon I saw her fight five guys, one after another!" the sweating man said.

"Shh!" everyone in the room hissed. Squid did too.

The man glistening with perspiration stood up and said, "I have a right to speak. I knew her better than anyone here. We drank together every night through June."

A man in front of Squid stood up. He swayed a bit and slurred his words. "All you did was steal her money, you thug!" The swaying man's friend grabbed him by the shoulder and pulled him down.

The rest of the crowd murmured scattered phrases. "Respect, respect. This is a funeral. We're in church."

"Well, anyway," the kitchen worker continued, "she'd come to eat food here at the mission sometimes. It wasn't always easy. Sometimes we had to throw her out. But today we wanted to give people time to remember the good parts of her life. She wasn't shy, and she had a good laugh, and that's all I have to say 'cause I didn't know her as long as some of you did."

The kitchen worker sat down so quickly, several people flinched. Then Rachel got up. "I don't like talking in front of groups . . ."

Squid had never seen her nervous before. She was twisting the ring on her finger around and around as fast as she could. "But Peaches and I used to joke around a lot . . . on the days she didn't punch someone in the face across the table." Everyone in the hot room laughed, because everyone loved Rachel. They would have laughed with her if she had read the want ads from yesterday's paper, if it would have encouraged her. Her blue eyes began to sparkle a bit, and Squid realized she was about to cry. Squid had never seen her when she was not smiling. He wondered what would happen if he were to rush up and put his arm around her.

"But I always wondered why she was called Peaches." Rachel faltered a bit, twisting the ring around her finger as if her life depended on it. "I mean, she was always punching somebody, and the men treated her like dirt, and all her clothes were black, and she wasn't exactly into all the feminine frills." Rachel paused a moment and made eye contact with each person in the room. Each person felt at that moment as though Rachel was their best friend. She took a moment to look directly at Squid. "And I have heard people make fun of her name, saying she's got the opposite of a peach complexion or that she's more a nut than a fruit and all that other stuff. But you know, I think she gave that name to herself. I think she did it without realizing it—that somewhere inside her was the spark of that kind of person, that wholesome, feminine person. You know, she really was a peach of a human being. That is what I think of her. That is what I will remember about her."

Rachel sat down very quickly and let out a solitary high sob and put her head in her hands. Every person in the room leaned forward, as if they might help protect this fragile goodness. At that moment, Larry marched down from the back of the room along the side wall and sat down beside Rachel. How did he get in without Squid hearing him? He laid his sombrero on the pew like a gentleman and put his other arm around her. Squid felt for the bat beneath his pants. He wanted to break that arm in a hundred pieces for daring to touch Rachel. Rachel continued to sob. Larry looked around the room and then looked directly at Squid. Squid looked back for awhile, but Larry never broke the gaze. Everyone else in the room noticed it also. Everyone in the room turned around and looked at Squid.

Squid looked down. His face burned. Unc would think he was very stupid for being here.

The kitchen worker stood up and said, "Let's sing another song and we'll let some other people talk."

As people fumbled with the musty hymnbooks, Squid quietly got up and gently opened the door. *I've got to talk to Unc*, he decided.

Squid limped a few blocks to Unc's corner then dropped his head and sighed. Jason was sitting on a milk crate next to Unc again, talking away about some philosophy or something. "Doesn't that guy have work to do?" Squid said out loud. "Isn't he supposed to be, like, cleaning the tables, or sorting out clean socks? Shouldn't he be at Peaches's funeral or something?" Squid slowed down and shuffled and limped his way to Unc's place.

Jason stopped in the middle of his speech and offered Squid his milk crate. "Squid, what happened to you? You look like you just had an accident. Sit down here, man, and rest a bit."

"You don't get off that easy!" Unc shouted at Jason. "The Bible is great literature, perhaps the greatest literature of all time, but you are attempting to make it something that it cannot be. You are merely deceiving yourself."

"Look, Unc." Jason had rested one knee on the sidewalk. "You have read a lot more than I have. But we both agree that words are loaded with power. Words are not meaningless combinations of letters to be used to manipulate people, or worse yet, to taunt them. Words can give a blessing, or a curse—"

"Listen, Unc, I really need to talk to you. It's really important." Squid bent over and held his stomach.

"Just a moment, grandson," Unc lifted his hand. "Yes, Jason, words are powerful. But you can find words that cleanse and ennoble in *King Lear* or *The Illiad* or *The Epic of Gilgamesh*. You have taken one chunk of human experience and tried to make it the standard for all people, for people like me that don't want it to shape their lives."

"Right, Unc. But let me say what my experience has been. You see, when I open the Bible, it's not like reading anything else. It's not like reading Dante or Plato. It offers me more than philosophy or science or sociology or literature could ever offer. That's why I can say that I believe the Bible, because I have found it to be so. It's not just true for me; it's flaming truth. It has been true for A, B, C, and D, and I trust it to be true for E, F, and G. In a way that doesn't happen anywhere else, the stories in the Bible become my story, no, in a way that I cannot describe. Now wait a minute, Unc—this is important to me, Unc—I become a part of its story." Jason acted as if he had just discovered something. "That's it, Unc." He shook his fist in front of his own face. "I become a part of *its* story."

Squid moved his milk crate back a bit so that he was less visible. He sighed a loud sigh and adjusted the bat under his pants.

Jason kept going. "As I read, I become a part of David's story. What a story—a young man who was promised to be king finds himself homeless and on the run in a strange land. His words to God and God's words to him become my words to God and God's words to me."

"And I feel the same way about Eugene O'Neill," Unc interjected. Sweat was running down his red face.

Jason continued. "I saw the same thing happen with my father. He became a part of Job's story. My dad had a tough time. But the random setbacks in my dad's life didn't seem random anymore. He would call himself Job. Then even his troubles took on a larger and deeper meaning. That is what I mean. When you open the Bible, or even if you don't, some verse or phrase may touch you at just the right time. That word, that verse, may help your whole life crystallize in a completely new way, in a way that you never intended. Random occurrences, stupid things, layers of experience—all of it becomes a part of the river of time . . . of promise." Jason clenched his fist and stared at it as he talked. "Sometimes it only takes a word—a word—for the lost parts of your life and heart to realign and become, like, significant."

"Ah, significance." Unc lifted a new bottle. "That is a word full of sound and fury and signifying, well, not much. I've become part of the Bible too—Ecclesiastes." Unc looked at Jason with an ugly sneer. "Emptiness, emptiness, all is emptiness." Unc leaned back and his face relaxed a bit. "Thank you, young man, for sharing your experiences from your particular subculture, which are far removed from Squid and me and our squat. I'm sorry to say that your experiences do not apply to me."

"Unc, I really, really have to talk to you. When do you think you'll be finished?" Squid tried to keep his voice from sounding like a whimper.

"I'm so sorry, Squid. I'm getting up to go." Jason smiled a disarming smile directed at Squid and dusted off his jeans as he stood up.

"Just think about this," Unc said as he looked up at Jason. "Isn't all your kindness and your words about God a little bit like the worst of the nineteenth-century missionaries' coming into our culture and imposing a view that destroys our own?"

"I can only say what is true, and I believe there are some things that are true. I'm only *imposing* on you if the words aren't true. See ya, Squid." Jason walked away slowly.

"Yeah, right, words that are true." Unc said the sentence with scorn as Jason walked away. Unc took another drink and wrapped the sheet around him more tightly. "You know, grandson, I think he is really progressing. A few more days of conversations with me, and I think we will have him as confused and shattered as you and I are. Now, tell me how my brave warrior is doing."

"Unc, I think I have to leave or something. I don't think Saw is going to just scare me or beat me up or leave me with a scar. I think he is going to kill me or something."

Unc took another drink.

"No, I think he's going to do something worse than kill me. I think he's going to skin me or stuff me or cut my legs off and sew them on my head while I'm still alive or something crazy that I can't even say. He's into black magic and sicko things, and they've probably got an underground cult or a secret society or something. You know how paranoid I am, Unc. I think Larry is after me and that is why he is stealing things from me. And I thought Squeaky and Cheese were OK but they just tried to kill me, Unc, with tire irons. I'm serious, Unc. Squeaky and Cheese, for Pete's sake. They tried to beat the life out of me. These people are not just like Ping-Pong balls; they are like evil or something. If Squeaky and Cheese are trying to crack my skull, maybe there are other nuts out there looking for me right now. Unc, my stomach has hurt really bad all day. It's feels like someone that doesn't like me is squeezing it real hard. I'm all tied up in nuts."

"You mean knots?"

"Yeah, that too."

"Ah, Cheese. I remember him when he first got here. He was just another runaway kid, maybe thirteen or fourteen years old. Now just a few years have passed, but he looks so much older. It's all the stuff he's doing to himself. Did you ever have a dog, Squid?"

"I did, but it died real soon and I don't want to talk about it."

"We had a dog when I was a kid, and it stayed with us through a lot of troubles. It was a young puppy when I was a kid, and by the time I was a teenager, it was old. It would limp around with arthritis, just like an old man. That's what it is like watching these kids come in here and live in the squats. It's like watching dogs age. They get old so quickly. They die at twenty-eight and they look like they're fifty. Cheese is like that."

"You're not exactly on the healthy fast track either, Unc."

Unc ignored the comment. His voice got more theatrical. "The pictures of the stars at the newsstands make it seem as though they never age, but the portraits of Dorian Gray are here in the attic, here in the squats, aging horribly, and those stars don't even know it."

"Unc, please help me. I'm in deep trouble and I start talking about Squeaky and Cheese and you're talking about some Dorian Gray guy in the squats that I don't even know."

"Calm down, grandson, we will sort it out."

"Unc, I was really smart and I got in an ambulance to get away from Squeaky and Cheese. I almost wanted to stay there, but I jumped out. Do you think a doctor could have helped me today?"

Unc rubbed his knees and groaned. "You and doctors, Squid. You always think they are going to save you. You are in such a strange inner place today, my son." Unc looked up and bellowed in his Shakespearean voice, "'God and the doctor we alike adore / But only when in danger, not before. . . .' That's from an old English poet, my son."

"I don't know what you are talking about, Unc. I just know I am in deep trouble."

Unc shifted to take advantage of the little bit of shade provided by the tree of heaven. "We are being baked alive here on this sidewalk." He smiled at Squid. "We're like two strips of Chinese squid in a wok here, grandson. The aging process is accelerating today. Listen, Squid, do you have any more money? I've gotten a little bit, even a dollar from Jason, but I need a little bit more to have refreshments for tonight."

"Unc, I'm really serious about what's happening to me. I think that everywhere I turn, this gang of secret wackos are slicing up people and animals and doing their little satanic things, and they are after me. I can't go to the park or to the mission or to my own place. They are, like, everywhere and they are going to take me to Saw. I was in his apartment, Unc, and I don't want to ever see that guy alone. I have this weird feeling that if he ever got me alone in some dark place, he would skin me—take my skin off like he does to all the pets he has stolen from the neighborhood. Those aren't just stories. I'm scared, Unc, really scared. I'm not just talking—these aren't just words. The truth is that I'm not that good at standing up to people. I act mad when I'm really scared. Usually I get cold feet, and this guy really scares me. I mean really."

"No, no, no, Squid, you don't have to convince me. I have no doubt that Saw is capable and willing to take his pound of flesh from you, literally. But do you have some small change, perhaps? You see, someone threw a token for the subway in my cup today, and I already have a token. Look, give me your money, and I will give you this token, and you can get out of here, something you should have done early this morning." Unc held up the copper-colored token for Squid. "You see, it's all so easy, and I get my liquification."

Squid sighed and fished a handful of change out and gave it to Unc.

With great ceremony, Unc handed Squid the token. "Here is your ticket to freedom, my warrior. Remember, you and Saw are alike in one way. Don't forget that you cheated him. To protect his name, he has to cheat you back in spades. I just think that he enjoys doing things like this way too much. Use the token. Now we both can be happy. I can drink . . . and you can live."

"I'm not using it. I have something I have to do tomorrow morning."

"Look, Squid. People have been coming by here and talking. Saw has more connections than I thought. Instead of just doing his small-time drug deals and petty intimidations, he now collects money on squats. He's a verified squatter landlord. He walks into places with some little gang of people and says that he owns the squat. He asks for rent from everyone there. If they don't pay it, he has his group of small-time thugs beat them up. They come in with pieces of iron and beat up somebody. Don't you think you ought to leave, grandson?"

"I've got things I have to do, Unc. You said that I ought to be brave."

"Squid, just remember that there are two kinds of people here. There are people like Rachel and our friend Jason, who will get attention if they call the police, who live in a legal place, who have nice teeth, who smell nice. They walk around the street and they have friends, family, and institutions standing behind them that will make sure nothing happens to them. Wherever they go, all those institutions are wrapped around them like armor. They're not really being very brave being here.

"You, on the other hand, are not that kind of person, Squid, and Saw knows it. He can have you beaten up and no one will ever even know about it. You can even dis-appear and everyone will think that you have just drifted to another neighborhood. No one will check up on you. No one would check up on me. Rachel and Jason will never understand that. Your lack of a safety net wouldn't even enter their mind. But Saw knows it. In fact, I think he is sniffing around our squat now with designs to become our landlord. Wouldn't that be delightful? Having Saw or one of his little quislings visit us every week? Squid, why don't you just get out of here for awhile?"

Squid wrapped his hands up into his shirt as tight as he could and said nothing.

Unc took a swig from his bottle and laughed a husky alcoholic laugh. Squid didn't think it was a kind laugh. "What a rickety claptrap contraption the world is. You, Squid, obviously have something you need to do to be trustworthy. You want to be trustworthy to someone special, and that desire will make you risk great harm." Unc leaned back. "That is very admirable. You want that trust to tie you together. A kind of trust ties you and me together. A failure of trust has created a glitch in the contraption for you and Saw. Somebody didn't do what he said he'd do. Really, that person was you. Everyone in this neighborhood is always asking, 'Can I trust him?' Or 'Will he do what he says he'll do? Will he pay what he says he'll pay? Will he deliver?'"

"Are you coming down on me, Unc? I can't handle all this today, Unc."

Unc didn't stop to listen. His voice only got louder at the interruption. "Trust is what lets you know that when you put your money down on the counter, they'll give you a drink. Trust is what a landlord gives a tenant, believing he will pay the rent. Trust is what keeps Wall Street moving, twenty blocks away. Trust is what builds huge corporations, and lack of trust makes them crumble." Unc's voice was loud enough now to be heard across the street. "Lack of trust makes nations invade nations, war and chaos, the proud badge of our failure to be responsible with what we say. Still, trust provides the pins and wires for our society to stick together"—Unc gestured expansively toward Squid—"lurching toward our own tailor-made Armageddon."

"Are you talking about the way I walk? I'm only lurching because of my broken toe, Unc. That was Bonehead's fault."

Unc's eyes rested on Squid and he gave him a bleary smile. "Well, everyone makes their choices. I'm choosing to go get some backup hydration and then read some Milton. You need to keep moving, and to be quite honest, you're not the healthiest person for me to be around this afternoon. Take care, grandson." With groans Unc raised himself up and started ambling toward the far corner.

Squid looked around and started moving too. He did not move toward the subway station. He turned toward the mission. "Someone there will talk to me," he muttered, "even if it's Jason."

Everything on the street was roasting. Squid couldn't put his hand around the chain-link fence because it was too hot. Fewer people were walking around. Most of the squatters and the homeless had migrated to the park or someplace close to a tree. The heat made Squid want to punch someone. When he thought about Cheese and Squeaky, he felt as though some invisible hand had reached inside his stomach and squeezed his intestines. Somehow he would get back at Larry and Molly. He wished he could whack Bonehead with Bonehead's own stick because he was snooping around his room. It was Bonehead's fault that he was limping right now anyway, the bonehead.

For a brief moment, he felt a pang of remorse as he thought about Bonehead taking care of the baby squirrel in the box and carrying her around in his pocket in this heat. Bonehead was probably still waiting for him in the park right now. But he didn't have time to think about that. He didn't want people to see him on the street. "I hope they think I died in the emergency room," Squid said. Of course, Larry had seen him at the funeral or whatever it was. Squid swallowed hard and tasted the fear in his mouth. This fear somehow floated around Saw's skinned squirrel and his knife and those stupid little satanic objects and Molly's nose that looked like it had been broken about twenty times. But this fear was deeper than that. And wider. More like a fog that covered everything.

Panic bubbled up in Squid's stomach. He looked around to see if there was anywhere around he could just bend over and hide. He leaned against a trash can and inhaled a wave of urine and rotten fruit. The heat felt like a thumb down his throat and almost made him gag.

In the next building, Squid found some metal stairs that led down to a basement door. He jumped over the iron fence and went down below the street level to get out of sight. His brain felt like a subway car again with too many people trying to get in. He squatted on the ground and rolled his hands up into his shirt. Fear squeezed his stomach more and more tightly. Squid let out a solitary yelp like a hunted animal cornered by dogs. He squeezed his eyes tight to keep anything like tears from coming. With his eyes closed he felt something like a shadow of hatred laying its hands on his shoulder.

"Get out of here, ya junkie," someone shouted through an open window in the basement, "or I'll call the cops!" Squid couldn't see who was speaking because of the screen. "Sorry, sorry, I must have come to the wrong building. You're not . . ." Squid searched for someone's name. "You're not Ratchet, are you?"

"I'm dialing the cops right now!"

Squid climbed up the stairs and jumped over the fence. He stopped and adjusted his shirt and the little bat under his pants. He limped straight ahead, and when he turned the corner, he saw the mission. The street was almost empty. Just half a block more and somehow he would feel safe. No one was outside.

Unc thought it was funny that Squid came to the mission so often now. It took a long time for Unc to persuade him to come. Squid remembered the time when he first met Unc and Unc had him go to some special grant program at the big Salvation Army place on Fourteenth Street. It was a little out of his neighborhood. Of course he would have never gone without Unc.

They went into a big room with a lot of people waiting around. They were all going to get food or something, or at least that's what Squid remembered. Everyone had to take a number at the door out of a plastic dispenser like they had at the ice cream store when he was a kid. A lady with a bossy voice walked around with a clipboard. "No names for this program please, just numbers!" she shouted. She had glasses on a string around her neck and would put part of the earpiece in her mouth every time someone tried to talk to her. Squid got his number, 257. He stayed close to Unc and finally grabbed two vacant folding chairs against the wall.

"This is going to be a long wait," he said to Unc as he bit his thumb and watched the lady with the clipboard berate some mother with two kids who went to the wrong worker. "I may not be able to do this, Unc."

Unc was wrapped in a sheet and blissfully reading a cheap murder mystery. "Fortitude, grandson, fortitude. This program is really for illegal immigrants, but we'll fit right in, I think."

Hours later, the bossy lady directed Squid to an intake worker. The intake worker was a young woman, hardly older than Squid. "Hi," Squid said as he sat down.

The young woman didn't answer. She didn't even look up. She had been doing this all day. She had a form she was filling out. It had the number 257 at the top. Without looking up, she began to speak to Squid. "You are part of a special program for people without proper documentation. You will not be asked your name, but you are required to give other information in order to participate. This information is confidential and will not be used against you in any form." She spoke in monotone, as if she were reading it from the form.

"OK," Squid said.

"Question number one. This question is optional. What is your ethnic background?"

Squid looked around at the bossy lady, who was scolding Unc because he was wearing a dirty sheet. Unc was refusing to look up from his murder mystery.

"Um, what are the options?"

The young woman let out an exasperated sigh and said, "Caucasian, Hispanic, African American, Asian, Native American, or other."

Squid thought about what his mom had told him. "I don't really know," he finally said and smiled at the lady, trying to get her to look at him.

She proceeded in a monotone. "I will not put an answer, then, since the first question is optional."

Squid blushed. He felt like he was back in school and failing a test.

"How many members are in your family?"

Squid moved nervously in the folding chair. "Zero," he finally said.

"That is not one of the options for an answer for this question." The woman still had not looked up at him once. Did he smell that bad? Was he a piece of garbage? Was his breath that bad? Didn't she notice that he was young, probably just a little younger than she was?

"No, wait then. One. Well, two, counting my mom. But I don't know where she lives. No, then just say one. But, wait, my uncle's here with me, or he is like my uncle. Does he count?"

Still monotone. "Is he a member of your family and does he live with you?"

"Yes . . . no. Yes. Put down two." Squid started scratching his head nervously. He wished Unc would help him out here. But Unc was serenely reading his mystery novel as the bossy lady stood over him and shouted at him. She had gotten the security guard over there with her. Everyone was getting quiet and watching Unc's astonishing refusal to acknowledge the lady with the clipboard. Everyone was happy to see him do that.

"What is the address?" The flatness in her voice continued.

"Um, well, I don't know. This is kind of embarrassing. You see, it's a squat, and it doesn't have a number on the front, so I've never really known what the address is. I'm sure it has one, I just don't think anyone that lives there now knows what it is."

The lady kept looking down at her paper without saying anything. Her pen was motionless. Squid could feel her irritation.

"Well it's on Ninth Street." Squid wanted her to start writing again. He wanted to get out of there. Unc had now stood up and was saying something in a loud theatrical voice. Squid thought he was quoting Shakespeare. Everyone waiting in the folding chairs was electrified. The bossy lady was still shouting, and the security officer was holding his hands up, trying to calm everyone down. "It's 257 East Ninth Street," Squid blurted out.

The young woman's pen still did not move. Squid thought that she might think he was making fun of her. She proceeded talking without writing anything. "Define *squat*, please. Is this single-family housing or part of a multi-family housing complex?"

"What?" Was she kidding Squid? The security officer was now pulling Unc toward the door as Unc continued to gesture dramatically at the bossy lady. The bossy lady was pointing her finger at Unc and had not stopped yelling. Squid leaned way down until his head was almost on the table. He was trying to get this young woman to look at him. She knew what he was doing and refused to make eye contact. She stared only at the paper and waited for his answer. "Look, lady, I live in a squat. You better learn what a squat is, because it is in your neighborhood. I live with my uncle there, who looks after me and cares for me. He's the one in the toga over there being pushed out of your crummy room. We're people who live right next to you and walk on the same streets, and you walk by me and look right through me. So if it makes you feel any better, I am 257 and I live at 257 East Ninth Street and I am 257 years old and my telephone number is 257-257." Squid grabbed the form she was writing on and folded it once, then twice, very neatly. "Thank you—from both me and my uncle."

Unc had now been completely ejected from the room. Squid rose and followed him out to the street.

Squid smiled as he remembered his bad experience with people who were supposed to help him. That poor young woman probably had her own problems. It took him awhile to get used to the mission. But now he loved coming to the mission, and here he was at the steps. He tried the door and it opened. He walked into the dining room area. The place where they gave out the food had that smell of old soup and Clorox and wet wood and dirty mop water. People were in the kitchen, washing pots. The room was almost as hot as the street outside. He could hear the workers through the window in the kitchen wall where they passed the food. A tape was playing some churchy music, women with really sweet voices harmonizing about whoever was thirsty.

Rachel usually wasn't around in the afternoon, but Squid didn't care. He wanted to talk to anybody. Even Jason. Squid went to the door of the kitchen. When he opened the door, he saw two younger men and one older man scrubbing pots and stacking them. But there on the side of a table and facing him was Rachel. Squid rolled his hands up in his T-shirt and walked over to her. Rachel had a row of kitchen knives and long serving forks in front of her. The kitchen knives had wet wooden handles and dirty metal blades. She was picking each knife or fork up in turn and drying it with a towel.

"Are you enlarging your T-shirt or just warming up your hands after a snowball fight outside?" Rachel grinned and hunched her shoulders up as if she were freezing.

"Rachel, I have to talk to someone. Do you have a minute?" Squid wanted to say something clever about making a snowman or something, but nothing came to mind.

"Sure, Squid, just warm your hands by the fire and tell me what's happening while I finish these knives."

"Could we talk at one of the tables just for a minute? I don't want to take up much of your time. You see, I don't really feel comfortable around knives. I have some really bad memories from when I was a kid." Why did he say that?

Rachel smiled again and made his words seem like a natural thing to say. "Sure, Eskimo." She put down the knife in her hand and turned to the other workers. "I'm talking to Squid in the dining room." Rachel went through the door and sat down at the first table next to the window. They were far enough away so that the workers couldn't hear them, but Squid could watch them. On the tape, some man with a soft high voice was singing something about coming to the waters.

Squid sat down and looked around the room. Rachel had her auburn hair pinned back in a little ponytail. Her white blouse looked fresh and crisp, and the short sleeve was rolled up a time or two on her arm. Squid knew he couldn't talk if he looked directly into Rachel's clear blue eyes, the color of the sky. There was an awkward silence. Squid started chewing on one of his thumbs, thought better of it, hid his thumb back in his T-shirt, and blushed.

He blurted out the first thing that came to mind. "I used to be really scared to come to the mission."

Rachel smiled her inclusive smile and rolled her eyes. "I'm still really scared to come here sometimes. There are so many funny things going on, I'm scared I'll laugh too much."

Squid couldn't help but smile. "One of the reasons even Unc doesn't know about. You know, I never went to church as a kid. I do remember loving a bunch of stories in a Bible book at a doctor's office once, even though I never saw the doctor. The stories were all about Abraham and Joseph and stuff. It had some great pictures." Squid stopped talking for a moment to get his bearings. "So, anyway, I never went to church here when I first got here. That was before I met Unc. I was wandering around the park and sleeping by the river."

Squid leaned forward. "One day this van drives up and all these people get out. They're real friendly and some are talking Spanish and some are talking English, and they give me this sandwich and little booklet with cartoons about God and heaven and hell." Why was he telling her this? Squid never knew why he said what he said to Rachel. "So they are really nice but there are a lot of them, and one of them is putting his arm around my shoulders, which freaks me out a little because I'm a little antsy about people I don't know touching me and everything. So it's not bad or anything, and they tell me about their church and how much fun it is, and they laugh a lot, even at my jokes and all."

Rachel listened silently.

Words kept tumbling out. "So anyway, they tell me how much God loves me and if I have any problems, he will save me. And they are all moving closer and closer to me, which is beginning to make me really uncomfortable, although they are really nice to me and gave me a sandwich and all. So they are moving really close to me and I am getting nervous, and they say they want to pray for me, so I kind of say OK. And then they all lay their hands on me, which really freaks me out but they don't know it, and the one who put his arm around me begins to pray for me in the deep voice right there in the park. I'm really embarrassed, and I don't like all these people I don't know with their hands on me."

Squid couldn't stop now. "So I start to try to get away, but all their hands just press harder on me, and the man with the deep voice is praying really loud that God deliver me from all my problems. And when I try to move, they won't let me move, and I'm starting to feel all claustrophobic and sweaty."

Squid looked at Rachel and smiled. "And then I know it's not right but I start to curse at them to let me go because nobody is going to mess with me, but their hands just hold me tighter, it's got to be ten or fifteen of them, and they say, 'Praise the Lord. It's the demons coming out of him.' And they all start praying really loud and in some other language, and I start cursing really loud, and they keep saying, 'Praise the Lord, there's a lot of demons and they are all coming out of him.' I was freaking out, Rachel, and I was cursing and kicking and slugging those nice, scary people, and I kicked the man with the deep voice in his groin and he stopped praying really fast and I ran away, cursing at them like crazy." Squid took a deep breath. "So that's one reason I was scared to come here, 'cause I was afraid the workers would put their hands on me again and say I had the devil in me and all that kind of thing."

He finally looked at Rachel to see if she was going to hate him. She looked at him with her blue eyes, but she wasn't frowning. She was trying to hold back a laugh. But it was a good laugh, a laugh that somehow made Squid feel included, not the way Unc laughed on a drunk day. Finally the laugh came out in a big outburst, and Rachel looked down and her shoulders were shaking.

Squid couldn't help but smile too. He felt heavenly. Rachel was laughing with him. All of a sudden, it did seem kind of funny to Squid too. Rachel looked up at him and exploded again and put her face in her hands while her shoulders continued shaking. Finally she looked up and a tear came down from one eye. Squid would have done anything for her at that moment. He would have walked through a wall.

"Squid, that is the funniest thing I have ever heard in my entire life." She called him Squid. She was laughing with him. He was laughing with her. The more he thought of that, the more he laughed. "You mean, the more you cursed at them and tried to get away, the more they thought you had demons and the harder they prayed?"

Squid was laughing now and nodding his head. He didn't know why.

"And the man stopped praying once you kicked him?"

Squid nodded his head, wheezing with laughter.

Rachel wiped the tear from her eye and started to calm down. "Oh, that is rich, that is really, really rich. I'm sure they thought they did you a ton of good, Squid."

"Yeah, well, they scared me to death and I just about peed in my pants, and I almost never came to the mission . . . but I am glad I did." A wave of emotion swept over him, and he almost choked when he tried to speak again. He couldn't speak, and Rachel didn't seem to have anything to say either. He could hear the music playing in the kitchen and the pots and pans clanging and that was about it.

The moment had passed. Squid didn't know what to say now. Finally he said, "Unc thinks the most important verse in the Bible is one where God speaks and some people think that its just thunder. He says that everything in life depends on the interpretation, even in the Bible. It could be God's voice, and then again, it could be just thunder. Is that verse in the Bible?"

Rachel had calmed down. She made it seem natural to talk about God. "I think I know the verse you are talking about, but I don't think it is a key verse. Like I said this morning, I think the verses that talk about God's character and personality in the Bible are a lot more important. The word used in the Bible for someone's character or essence is indicated by their name. That's why Moses wanted to know the name of God. He was really asking, 'Who are you?' Squid, later God tells Moses more about his name. Do you know what the first two qualities are when God proclaims his name? He is merciful and gracious. Isn't that wonderful?" Rachel had taken on that earnest tone that Unc disliked so much. Somehow Squid didn't mind.

"Rachel, is there a place in the Bible where it talks about three angels or something? Is that in the Bible?"

"Well, I think three angels came to Abraham and Sarah, and the promise was so wonderful and incredible that it made them laugh. There's that idea of names again. They named the son of that promise *Isaac*, or 'laughter.' And think of Abraham. Can you imagine having no children from your legitimate wife and being old and telling all your friends that God had called you a new name that meant 'father of a multitude'? Don't you think people laughed? Can you imagine telling your friends your new name is 'father of a multitude' when you don't have one child from your legitimate wife? Talk about humiliating."

"I know more about Abraham Lincoln than that other guy, but I remember that Abraham guy's picture in a book real clearly, and he had a long beard and a robe. But those angels, do you think there are really things like that? I mean, do you think there are really angels that come to people to wish them well, or do you think that it is just poetry or something?"

Rachel took a minute to think about the question. "No, I think that there really is an unseen world, that there is a lot more going on than we can touch with our hands." She put her hand down flat on the table with a thump.

"Yeah, I think I know more what you mean today than I did yesterday," Squid said. He sat through another long, awkward pause as he tried to sort out what he really wanted to say. "You know what my favorite verse is?" he finally asked. "I learned it here. It's when Jesus says, 'My God, my God, why have you forsaken me?' I can understand that. Now that makes sense to me."

He could tell Rachel didn't quite understand him. She started from another direction. "Satan's name has a meaning or essence too. It means 'accuser.' Jesus says that Satan is a liar and a robber and a killer. He wants to rob you. He wants to make you feel forsaken. He wants to take your courage, and he wants to take your essence, your name. That is what he is like. He would take the skin off your back if he could."

"Is Satan like an angel too?" Squid knew he was out of his element. He started wishing he could turn the conversation to the Yankees or something.

"Well, yes, kind of. But Satan wishes you harm. He's a robber. Have you ever felt robbed or cheated or scared? That's what Satan wants to do."

"Look, I have felt all of those things *today.*"

"Well, that's where God comes in," Rachel continued. "You see, he promises to give you a new name, a new character. That's why he told Simon that he was going to start calling him 'Rock.' And even though Simon wavered all over the place, he *did* become a rock." Rachel stopped and screwed up one side of her face, as if she were thinking really hard. "Well, finally anyway, he became like a rock. Nowadays we always talk about identity, like who you are and stuff like that. But the Bible deals with that by talking about someone's name. You know, in the Bible, the name

Jacob really means 'cheater,' but later, Squid, God gives Jacob this really great name, a name of great dignity."

"Yeah? He gets another name?" In spite of himself, Squid started chewing on his thumb.

"Then at the end of the Bible, God even promises to give *you* a new name, which no one else will know except *you.*"

"God really says that?"

"Yeah, Squid, and it really is for real. It's not just talk."

Squid wrapped his hand back in his shirt again. "It's just that everything seems so jumbled today. Usually I just agree with what Unc says. He's so smart and I'm not. But I did something really wrong, and now I am in big trouble. I am really scared and there are things happening that make me know that I am in way over my head and out of my league. I don't even know why I am telling you all of this, but I know that Unc was right and that my life is all jumbled up like a bunch of Ping-Pong balls bouncing around. Do you think that's what life is? Do you think everything is just happening by chance, and stuff is just bouncing around like the lottery?"

"Well," Rachel was taking his thoughts very seriously and choosing her words carefully. "I think life *feels* like a bunch of Ping-Pong balls a lot of the time, but I don't really think that this feeling is the final word. You see, because I think there is a God who really is there, with a personality, a name—not just some floating spooky force out there." Rachel paused for a moment to find the right words. "Because of that, he gives us a name, a reason to be, a purpose. We are not just some invisible thing sitting on the sidewalk."

"Yeah," Squid said warmly. "I know what you mean. Did you talk to Jason about me? Did he tell you where he saw me today? Sitting on the sidewalk?"

"No, I haven't and he didn't. I changed my shifts around today so we can go to see the circus animals in the late night and I can still get some *beauty* sleep," she joked.

"Well, I don't know what to do next. I think I'm going to die today, and I want to kill about six people before I die, but you know, it's really that I'm so scared. That's really it. I'm scared because I'm angry and I'm angry because I'm scared." Squid took a big fresh bite of skin off his thumb. "Mostly I'm scared." Why was he saying this all to her?

The workers in the kitchen were laughing about something. Rachel did not turn around to see what the joke was about. She just stared quietly at Squid.

Squid couldn't look at her. "Ya see, I'm a nut job. My mom was a nut job, though not as bad as me. She made some poor choices, just like I do. The men she had around were . . . ," Squid faltered. He'd never talked about this to anyone, not even Unc. "Whew!" Squid looked over to the wall and blew out air, trying to get hold of himself. A long silence followed. This was not what Squid had planned. "I never want to go back to any of those places where I grew up," he said finally. "That's why I am here. Here I can just drift from place to place and no one knows me or cares. I'm like a ghost or invisible, and I don't have to talk or think about all those things that happened to me. But sometimes

I don't want to be invisible, like today, with you, or with . . . Jason. I can't believe I'm saying that. I don't know what I am saying."

Rachel stared at him with her hands folded on the table. As the silence continued, Squid's face became flushed and red. Rachel sat more quietly than he had ever seen her.

Maybe she's waiting to give her God a chance to work, Squid thought. All Squid felt at that moment was horrid remorse that he had said so much, that he had showed so much weakness, that he was so much more vulnerable to betrayal.

Finally Rachel quietly said, "I'm so sorry, Squid."

Squid wiped his nose with the back of his hand and rubbed his eyes with his fists as if he were ten years old.

After another long pause, Rachel continued, "I can only imagine what you've gone through, and I don't have any idea what has happened today. I don't need to know, Squid. But I do know that there is someone beyond me that knows you far better than I do or anyone else, even your mother."

Squid put his head in his hands. "Oh, please stop." This was too much. This was moving toward something or someone that he didn't want to face. "Don't say anything else about anybody's mother."

"Squid, I can't even begin to tell you how to solve your problems. I have no idea. But I can tell you about the one who helped me walk through all my problems. He is the one you mentioned before, who can understand even when you say you feel totally forsaken by God. His own family thought he was crazy, but he never made anyone feel like a zero, no matter who they were."

"I can't take this," Squid said, pressing his fists into his forehead.

"Squid, I won't force you to do anything, but I will tell you that when you turn to Jesus, it's like opening the door of your life. That's the best way to describe it. No matter what has happened to you today, he understands. It's like opening a door. Then he gives you a new character, your real name, so to speak. He never destroys who you have been but draws you to who you are to become. It's so real, Squid."

Squid looked down and rubbed his scalp over and over again.

The workers were stacking big pots in the kitchen. "Squid, can I pray for you?"

"No," Squid said quietly.

"Squid, would you close your eyes with me and just ask God for help?"

Squid leaned back and looked up at the ceiling. "Nope." He would do almost anything for Rachel, but he was not going to do that. He stared up at the ceiling and frowned. He had never prayed since he was with his mom, and he was not going to start now. He would say almost anything Rachel wanted him to, but he was not going to bow his head. Somehow he knew that if he did so, he would be doing something he couldn't change or go back on, like submitting to a drug dealer or a squatter landlord. He had never submitted to anything, he told himself, and he wasn't going to start now.

Rachel wasn't giving up. "I've learned that the most important question is not the *why* but the *who*. Who do you go to when you are in trouble?"

That question made sense to Squid. He thought of Unc. He thought of giving him four bucks this afternoon.

Rachel continued, "I'm telling you about a *who* for whom there is no problem too big. He paid a price so big—"

"No," Squid interrupted. He was not going to bow his head and pray, even if it was Rachel doing the praying. Suddenly a new thought slipped into his mind like a sparrow landing on an open window. What if there were something or someone as good as Saw was evil? Someone as right as Saw was wrong? Something even kinder than Saw was mean? For a moment, Squid almost half believed it as he sat in the mission. Why did he go to the mission instead of going to see Unc?

"Squid, you don't have to agree to anything, say anything, change anything. Just let me pray for you. That's all." Plates were being moved in the other room, but Rachel was speaking very quietly.

Something in Squid's mind said, *Don't do it, don't bow your head, don't give in to anything, don't yield to anything.* Then another voice in Squid's head said, *I'm going to do it. I'm going to bow my head, though it doesn't really mean anything.* Squid put his hands flat down on the table, and slowly, very slowly bowed his head.

Rachel started praying very earnestly, saying the words *Jesus* and *blessing* and *help Squid* over and over again. Squid didn't hear a word of it.

CHAPTER 10

THE FIRST THING that Squid heard when he bowed his head was a cry. It came from deep inside of him. Inside himself he saw a man stretched out like an insect on a board. His cry was terrible.

The next thing he felt was a clear warmth, vast and calm. It touched his stomach first; it was like the last bit of a wave at Coney Island gently touching his midsection. The water dissolved every knot in his intestines.

His next thought was, *Who would want to fight this? Of course I want to bow my head.* The gentle clarity spread to his heart, his arms, and finally his head. *This is like when you pour water on the twisted wrapping of a paper straw. It all unwinds.*

For the first time in a long time, Squid wasn't trying to forget. He was trying to remember. He remembered his mother, holding him in her arms. He wasn't rushing around to get away from someone or something. He was stopping so that someone could come to him. Someone patient—as good and vast as the sky.

What Squid felt were colors—deeper than deep, richer than rich colors. Blue, green, yellow, red. They didn't feel like stolen colors that just made him hungry, like when he was smoking weed. No, for once every hunger was satisfied, more than satisfied. He wouldn't dare try to possess these colors, only feel them as a gift from the one who was coming.

The special one came closer and liquid love poured all over Squid's body. It was lighter than liquid, better than the best breeze on a summer night on the roof, gentle, healing. Almost like fluid sunlight. *I do not deserve this*, Squid thought, and yet, at the same time, maybe for the first time in his life, everything, everything seemed so right. To refuse this gift would have been to fracture what was good and whole.

"Thank you," Squid said out loud as Rachel's voice droned on in the background. Whatever this was, he wanted more of it, and for once it felt as though it were right to want more. The lightness, the presence intensified all over his body, especially his bowed back. The goodness became deeper and deeper. Squid thought he might die of wanting more of it. He felt as though he were five years old, running along the beach. The hurting stomach was gone, the hatred was gone, the fear. Squid didn't feel as though his problems would go away. Not at all. But he sensed that someone, that special someone would walk him through and make things right no matter what happened. That someone was with him, and no words, no words were necessary.

"OK, then, you carry the load," Squid said out loud. Rachel didn't hear him and kept praying. The presence didn't do anything or say anything. The cloak of kindness and protection just stayed there all around him. That presence was enough for Squid. He just sat there quietly with his head bowed.

Rachel's voice went on and on. Finally, she came to a close. "In Jesus' name, amen."

Squid didn't raise his head or move. He didn't want to stop. The presence of goodness receded quietly and gently. Squid became more aware of the noise in the kitchen, the heat, the fans droning on. Finally he looked up.

Rachel was sitting there with her hands folded, unhurried.

"Wow," Squid breathed out. "What just happened?" Squid looked down at his hands. "I mean, I feel so much peace right now. I'm not scared. I don't want to kill anyone. There was, like, peace in this room."

Rachel just smiled and waited. Finally she said, "That's the Lord, Squid. You called on him and he answered."

"But I didn't really call on him. I didn't ask him for anything. I just bowed my head and all these things started happening. Rachel, it was so real. Realer than real. Is that how it happens?"

"I don't know, Squid. For me, I was hardly a teenager, but I was in my church, and I asked Jesus to forgive me of my sins, and I just asked him into my life. I'm no Einstein. I just did it, and Jesus came in. Now I just trust him. Did I tell you that *trust* and *belief* and *having faith* are all the same word in the Bible?"

"But wait a minute. I didn't ask Jesus into my life. I have all kinds of trust issues. I just bowed my head and all these things started happening—God or peace or angels or Jesus or something. I guess it was Jesus. There was this pinned-up man crying out . . ."

Rachel raised her eyebrows and shrugged her shoulders. "I don't know, Squid. God does things a lot of different ways. I don't think Paul was asking Jesus to come into his life when Jesus came to him and just knocked him to the ground. Maybe God is trying to show you in a really strong way that it's not so much what you do in life as what is done for you. Maybe that's the way God is going to do it for you. But I guess somehow, someway, you have got to respond. It's like receiving a gift. But whatever happened to you, in the end, it won't matter much unless you trust in him and what he's given."

"Mmm." Squid had run out of words. The workers in the kitchen started throwing water at each other and racing round the kitchen table. "I gotta go now." Squid slid across the seat of the bench and the bat under his pants hit the leg of the table with a bang. For once, Rachel didn't make any jokes. "I'll see you early in the morning at our meeting place. Four o'clock. Good-bye."

Squid had to get out of there. His chest felt packed with too many emotions. He shut the door of the mission and felt the heat from the sidewalk and the buildings bake into his body. It felt so good. Squid breathed out hard and started limping down the street. On the one hand, he felt like Don Mattingly must feel after hitting a home run. He had never spent so much time with Rachel or talked to her so long. On the other hand, he was ashamed and embarrassed. Why had he told her about the knives? Why had he said anything about his mom? But most of all, he was stunned by that peace that came over him, that goodness that was there when he bowed his head. What was that about? What had happened?

For the first time all day, the sun felt good on Squid's face. He took a deep breath, sighed loudly, and let the muscles in his shoulders relax. He felt that, somehow, things were going to work out. His foot still hurt, but if he walked slowly and favored it, he felt fine.

Two young guys with spiked hair came up behind him. Each grabbed one of his arms. They yanked him into the open door of an old squat. Squid wished he were bigger so he could throw his weight around. The punks had chains on their belts that rattled as Squid struggled with them. The hallway of the squat building was cool and dark. The two punks pushed his back against the wall, and each started pulling his legs out from under him. Finally they got his rear end on the ground with his legs splayed out. Squid noticed that the floor was missing further down the hallway. In the darkness, it looked as though the hole dropped off into a basement.

Squirming, Squid looked up and saw a third man standing over him. Squid's eyes were not accustomed to the dark. The two punks were saying nothing, attempting to get his arms pinned to the wall as Squid struggled. Squid kept fighting and the third man got closer. Squid could tell in the dark that the third man was wearing cowboy boots. Squid looked up again and could tell the man had long blond hair. He looked like Custer.

"Ratchet!" Squid shouted. "Help me!"

Ratchet had his pet python, Snappy, draped around his arm. He reached his arm out to Squid's face and quickly wrapped Snappy around Squid's neck. Squid felt the cool, dry skin of the snake tighten slightly.

"What are you doing?"

Ratchet squatted down and looked into Squid's face. Ratchet spoke quickly and angrily. "Saw and all his little secret satanic friends want you bad, Squid. They are looking for you in the park, at your squat, even at the hospital. Now Saw is paying a good chunk of cash to anyone who hands you over to him. What did you do to him? I've never seen him so mad. But I tell you what. At least you can trust Saw's word. If he says he'll pay the money, he'll pay it. *You* will just take someone's money and keep it. No one can trust you. Now I'm just going to have to tie you up and hand you over."

Squid didn't say anything. Snappy was tightening his grip around Squid's neck. All the blood in his body felt stuck in his head, and he began to have trouble breathing.

It seemed like forever, but finally Ratchet unwrapped Snappy from Squid's neck with a curse and laid Snappy on the floor next to Squid. Ratchet pulled a roll of strong twine out of his back pocket. Squid knew what came next. Snappy was coiled on the ground next to Squid's foot. *Do the unexpected*, Squid thought. Squid gave the snake a swift kick. The snake slid down the hallway a few feet and dropped off into the blackness where the floor was gone.

Ratchet whirled around and shouted in a high voice, "Snappy!" To everyone's surprise, he took a few steps down the hall and jumped into the darkness. He totally disappeared. Both punks loosened their grip and looked with open mouths at the hole.

Squid didn't waste a moment. He yanked both arms down fast and slammed his hands against the floor. He jumped up, and the top of his head hit the bottom of the chin of one of the punks. He heard the punk's teeth clop together and felt the punk's head snap back from the impact. The other punk stood motionlessly as Squid limped quickly toward the outside door. The punks were so stunned they didn't even chase him as he escaped into the outdoor heat. *People, people, safety, safety,* he thought. Sure enough, there were plenty of people on the street.

Squid ran and limped as hard as he could, never looking back until he turned the corner. No one was there. But every place looked dangerous now. The street was dangerous. The park was dangerous. Squid wanted to talk to Unc. He needed some help. Squid headed toward his squat, thinking he could go the back way and head up the fire escape. Before he became visible to anyone in the front of his building, he veered off along the broken bricks and glass of the back way. It was lonely behind the buildings, and he knew that if he got caught there, he would be trapped. Squid picked his way through the garbage and looked around every corner. At one point in a messy lot, he could look through the buildings and see the Con Ed tower with its clock. Just four o'clock. He still had to hold out for twelve more hours to be with Rachel. That was like a whole day.

Finally he got to the back of his own building. It seemed deserted. Squid found a rusty, cracked kitchen table behind another building and dragged it over to the fire escape. Standing on the table, Squid could easily secure himself to the ladder. He climbed past the second floor without looking in. Before he got to the third floor, he stopped and rested. Just like this morning, he felt safe on the fire escape. He was like an animal, like a squirrel that has a much better advantage when up high. There he could see if anyone approached him. If someone came out the second-story window, he would climb in the third floor. If someone came out the third-story window, he would climb in the second floor. A squirrel makes sure to be always on the other side of the tree trunk from the dog chasing it. Squid could think like that and stay alive.

He didn't know what to expect when he went inside his own squat, so he paused and rested there in between floors on the fire escape. Squid looked out at the buildings around him and thought again about what had happened to him when he bowed his head at the mission. He wanted to thank something, or someone, for letting him get away from Ratchet, but he wasn't quite sure how that worked.

It was finally a little later in the day, and Squid was beginning to see a few more shadows in between the buildings. Things were even getting just a little bit cooler.

Squid could hear salsa music coming from an open window in a tenement building down from him. He could see someone barbecuing chicken on a roof about a block away. When the breeze was just right, he could even smell the barbecue. Squid could hear cars driving and honking on the street. When he was right next to them, he thought cars were really obnoxious. But up here, the sounds almost seemed like music. On another roof far away, a woman was hanging up laundry. The reds and whites of the tablecloths and sheets seemed to wave at him with the occasional breeze.

In the distance, Squid could see the housing projects rising above the tenement buildings. As he rested, he became aware of the hundreds and hundreds of windows he could see, both in the housing projects and in the tenement buildings. Through some of the open windows, he could sometimes actually see a figure pass by. There was a teenage girl looking out the window and shouting to her friend below. There was an old man who had a pillow on the windowsill, so he could rest his elbows on the pillow and look out for a long time. Squid thought of all the stories behind every single window. He thought about their meals, their laughter, and their fights.

Squid loved where he lived. Then he thought about the people in the squats—Unc, Chaos, Squeaky, Cheese, Larry, Ratchet. He thought again about eating Chinese food on the roof with Unc. Squid even felt that pang of remorse for Bonehead, who was probably still whacking stones and faithfully waiting for Squid in the park.

Soon all the abandoned buildings would be gone. People with money and nice teeth were already moving into the neighborhood because they thought it was the gritty and cool thing to do. Squid knew that squatters were not the first group to come and go in his neighborhood. Squid saw the German engravings on the building at the corner. A lot of Germans must have lived there at one time. He had friends that stayed in the abandoned synagogue down the street. A lot of Jews must have lived there at one time. He couldn't read the Spanish sign on the Pentecostal storefront. Puerto Ricans were getting pushed out now.

After all the fear and anger, Squid saw with great clarity that he and his friends would pass on. No one remembered or cared about the German immigrants, the Italians, the Jews, the Puerto Ricans, the Africans that lived in the tenement buildings. Squid realized that no one would remember Unc with his books, Bonehead with his little squirrel, or Squid with his bat down his pant leg. Everything was passing away. Their names would be forgotten. What would remain? The only thing that came to mind was that peace that Squid felt when he bowed his head in the mission room.

"I want to live," Squid said out loud to the city around him. "I don't just want not to die. I want to live. And I don't want to hurt anyone." He squeezed the iron ladder as hard as he could. "I'll do whatever it takes to keep from getting cut up." Squid climbed up to the third floor, making as little noise as possible. He stayed quiet outside the window for a long time. He could hear nothing. Finally he looked in and saw no one. He climbed through the window and stood still. Heat in the building had risen to the top floors, and the temperature was suffocating. Squid walked over to where Unc usually sat, resting on his blankets. On one of the blankets, Squid saw two three-by-five-inch cards. He picked them up and went over to the window to read them.

The first one said: "Squid, you know that in my life I did not get to the point of being a drunk in an abandoned building living with you by making courageous choices. Given the new circumstances, I have decided to disappear for a few days at least. You are on your own tonight after all. You know where I think you should go. You probably know where I am going. I will see you at some point. On the accompanying card, you will find my last message for you. UNC."

Squid saw that there was a quote for him on the other card, but he just folded it and put it in his pocket. He couldn't read anymore. Squid felt a wave of loneliness and fear wash over him. Even though Unc didn't really do much, he was at least someone to talk to. He gave Squid advice. Squid wanted to tell Unc about what he did to Ratchet and the snake. Unc would have been so proud of Squid the warrior. Now Squid felt that he had no one.

Squid went over to his mattress. All of a sudden, he was very tired, but he knew in his heart that he couldn't go to sleep here. As he walked over to the mattress, Squid smelled something before he saw it. Squid's bed was in the shadows, and he stood still for a moment to let his eyes become accustomed to the shade. He looked around the dark areas to see what smelled so bad. It was a familiar smell. There it was. On the corner of his mattress was something that shouldn't be there. It was the squirrel skin he had seen at Saw's house. It wasn't nailed to the board anymore, but as he looked closer, he could see where the nail holes had been. It looked roughly cut and smelled. Squid knew he had to think smart, but the first thought that came into his head was, *What if that squirrel were someone's mother?* But next he felt invaded, attacked. Some evil thing had come into his place. What if that evil thing had messed with his special hiding place? They or it or whatever might still be there. *It was Saw. He not only came in here, he's trying to psych me out. He's messing with my mind. He's trying to put one of his weird voodoo things on me too.* Squid checked the little flake on the loose brick where he hid his envelope, but it hadn't been touched.

Squid scooped up a plastic shopping bag from Unc's side of the room. Squid guessed that Unc had seen the squirrel before he wrote the note. Squid knew he should be running, but he didn't care. He gently picked up the smelly squirrel by a paw and placed it in the plastic bag. He tied the bag tightly and placed it by his bed. He lined up the side of the bag carefully with his mattress. He would try to do something to honor the poor squirrel's hide later on. Maybe he would bury it in that little park where Unc had taken Squid and Bonehead, the place they had found Flicker.

But there was no time to do that now. Just like at the mission, Squid felt a presence. But it was not gentle and kind. It was the presence he felt at Saw's place. Squid felt more in danger here than he did with Ratchet and his stupid fat snake. He stood still in the middle of the room to see if he could hear any slight noises or breathing in the other rooms. All he could hear were cars honking and starting and stopping on the street. Squid decided to walk down the stairs very quietly. If there were something there, he would rather face it than stay shivering with fear next to this little butchered squirrel in a bag.

Unc was always talking about courage. "Just do something, and the courage will come afterward," he'd say. Squid moved slowly toward the door and began to climb down the dark stairway. He placed his feet carefully so that he wouldn't make a sound. When he got to the second floor, he could see a few people sitting on the dirty mattresses and smoking some crack. They were facing the back windows and could not see Squid. He hatched a plan. Moving on to the stairway to the first floor, he quietly straddled the banister where the five steps were missing. The bat under his pants hit the banister hard and made a noise that echoed up the stairway. Squid had forgotten all about the bat. He should have pulled it out upstairs and used it for protection. Squid stayed quiet for a moment and then kept moving.

When he got to the main floor, he did not head for the front entrance. He went to the back of the hallway where it was very dark. Squid felt for a rusty old doorway and pulled it open a foot. It made a grating noise, but Squid stepped inside the door and shut it. He figured most of the squatters were too spaced out to check on the noise.

Now Squid was in total darkness, but he felt better. As far as he knew, no one had seen him go down into the cellar. He didn't think anyone was staying there. It was too dark and damp with too many rats. He descended the stairs. He had been down here one other time with Chaos when Chaos had a flashlight and they were looking for some lumber. He knew there was an empty room at the base of the stairs with an open concrete floor.

Squid felt his way to the bottom of the stairs and found the entrance to the room. Even though his eyes had become accustomed to the dark, he could see nothing. He sat down on the concrete floor and waited. He didn't care that it was so dark and he had no light. It might even be a line of defense for him. He could hear the basement door open if anyone came down there. As far as he knew, no one had seen him go down. Saw and his friends must be gone or waiting to catch him at the front of the building, where he usually entered.

At least it was cool in the basement. Squid was very, very hungry and could not face how lonely he felt. He lay down on the concrete and curled up in a fetal position. He found a little concrete ledge against the wall and rested his head on it. Uncomfortable, Squid moved around to try to find a good position for his head.

He did what he often did when he was trying to go to sleep. He remembered the last time he felt safe. He was in a rocking chair, sitting in his mom's lap. She was singing some kind of song to him and talking to him in between refrains. It must have been a quiet time in their life, in between boyfriends, before Sammy. Squid was maybe five or six years old.

Back and forth, back and forth, even the creak of the chair was comforting. Squid's mom had her arms around him, and he didn't have to do anything but lay still. Sunlight was coming in the bedroom window. The sheets on the bed were fresh and clean. He had just been given a bath and was wrapped up in a white terry-cloth bathroom towel that was still warm from the dryer. His mom's hair fell down her shoulders and touched his head. He was not hungry. He was not scared. His stomach didn't hurt. There were no other men in the house. All of his mom's attention was for him. He could tell that for once she was happy. She said his name with such sweetness and care as she sang her song. He could never quite remember what the song was.

Squid pushed some grains of sand off the cement ledge in the basement and moved his head to find some place where the tiny rocks weren't digging into his skull. He rolled over to the side and curled his legs up in a fetal position again. Finally sleep rested on Squid gently, as if someone who cared for him had adjusted a blanket up over his shoulders.

CHAPTER 11

SQUID DROPPED QUICKLY into a deep sleep. He dreamed he was floating in midair, watching everyone he knew climb down the fire escape behind his squat. He felt fine. He could see Unc and Rachel and Jason and Bonehead and a lot of others. They were like choreographed dancers in some strange musical, each stepping in unison to get to the bottom. He found that if he focused on any one person, he saw a scene in their life.

He looked at Unc at the top of the ladder. Unc looked cold. Somehow he was in one of those new subway cars that had air-conditioning blasting out all the time. He wrapped the sheet around him more closely and continued to read. On the cover of his dirty paperback were the words *Paradise* and *Dante*. He looked happy. He had a bottle in his front pocket peeking out from under his robe, and the car was almost empty. No one was bothering him. No one knew where he was. Unc was reading the book with great pleasure.

The loudspeaker in the subway car came on with a crackling sound. "Please listen to this important message," the speaker said. After the introduction, the muffled sound of words came through the speaker, but no distinct consonants. Unc couldn't understand a word of it. It didn't matter. Squid could see that he was on the L line headed for Rockaway.

Unc quietly took his bottle out and took a sip. He looked down at his book. No one else was in the subway car now. Squid knew how much Unc loved Dante. Unc began to read aloud in his deep, drunk theatrical voice. He didn't care who heard him. "All beings great and small / Are linked in order; and this orderliness / Is form, which stamps God's likeness on the All."

Unc looked up at the ceiling of the subway car rattling along the track. "How beautiful, how clear," Unc said, adjusting his head to find a corner for rest. "Beatrice says that." Unc's plan looked simple. He was living in the subway car. At Rockaway, Unc got out of the car and got in the car across the platform going back.

"I'm just like Huckleberry Finn, floating in a river of adventure, deep in the bowels of the city," Unc said as he put his book down on his lap and closed his eyes. "I hope Squid is OK by now." The subway started up and he drifted to sleep with the gentle rocking of the car. When Squid heard his own name in the dream, he wanted to reach out to Unc. He wanted to ask for Unc's advice, to tug on his dirty sheet like he had done so many times before. But it was as though he was watching a movie.

Squid was floating in air again and looking at the next person climbing down the ladder. It was Jason. Somehow he was watching him back at the mission. Jason pushed the plumber's helper one more time to clear the toilet. He stopped, straightened his back, and laughed out loud. "This is why I majored in marketing and minored in religion," he shouted to someone in the kitchen. "So I could be trained to clean toilets." He put the plumber's helper back on the floor. "I'm no bleeding heart," Jason mumbled. "Unc is wrong. And he's wrong about life too." He sounded to Squid as if he were trying to convince himself.

Jason flushed the toilet again. Then Jason got down on one knee there in the bathroom. "Well, God," he said out loud, "I'm ready to learn. I know you have instructed us to love one another. I just don't know how to do it in these circumstances." Jason got up and went to get a mop to clean up the floor. "I wonder what Squid's story really is," Jason said to no one. "I need to ask Rachel." Squid was a little bit embarrassed to see Jason kneel in a bathroom and pray. But he was a little bit happy to hear Jason mention his name. In his dream, Squid didn't feel jealous of him at all.

Squid was floating in air again and looking at the next person climbing down on the ladder. Rachel was on the ladder, but somehow she was really in front of the mission. It was all so sharp and clear in the dream. Rachel was outside with a tiny old lady with a shopping cart full of clothes. Even in the heat, the lady had two shawls on. She spoke with an Eastern European accent.

Then Rachel spoke: "No, no, no, clothing closet is tomorrow, not today. You have to come back tomorrow. *Tomorrow.*" Rachel said the last word much more loudly and emphatically and handed her a sheet with the times written on it. The lady refused to budge and tried to push her shopping cart forward toward the door. Rachel placed her leg firmly in front of the cart. "Ma'am," Rachel said sweetly with a smile and a twinkle, "I played football growing up with my brothers, and I really know how to block. You won't be able to get past me."

The lady may not have understood what Rachel said but she finally softened at Rachel's smile. She even gave Rachel a half-smile back. Rachel beamed in that way that included the old lady in the glow. As Rachel pointed one more time at the paper, she saw a shadow cover both her and the old lady. It was something big and round like an umbrella.

It was a sombrero. There was Larry standing over them both, smiling. "Larry, you scared us," Rachel said as the lady walked away. "You caught me somewhere between the siesta and the fiesta, and I'm ready to sing 'Desperado.'"

Larry smiled again and looked at the sun, which was sinking down closer to the buildings. "I have a message from Squid. Have you seen him?"

"Yeah," Rachel said, picking up an empty beer bottle on the stoop and throwing it away. "He was here this afternoon."

Larry moved closer to Rachel. "Squid can't meet you tonight. He's got to be gone for a few days."

In the dream, Squid was furious and tried to say something, but it was as though he was watching the scene from behind soundproof glass.

"Oh," Rachel said with a puzzled look.

"He was in a big hurry and asked me to tell you since he doesn't have a telephone or nothing."

"That's so sad . . . it sounded like so much fun. We were going to see the circus animals go through the tunnel." Rachel took a step back from Larry.

Larry took another step forward. "Yeah, Squid was sad too. What time did you say you were going to meet?"

"Oh, at four in the morning." Rachel backed up and picked up an old paper coffee cup. "We were going to meet at the parking lot around the corner. It would have been so much fun."

"Yeah, well, those things happen." Larry took a half step closer to Rachel.

Rachel backed up again and frowned at Larry. "So long, muchacho," Rachel said quietly and walked inside.

Squid felt so upset that he held his stomach in his dream, but he could do nothing. He was floating behind his building again, looking at the others climbing down his fire escape.

There was Bonehead. Squid felt that pang of remorse even in his dream because he had ditched Bonehead. Bonehead was still in the park. In the center of the park were about a hundred abodes—camping tents, cardboard boxes, and houses made out of blankets, broom handles, and old boards. Squid could see every detail. Some people had clear plastic sheeting draped to the iron fence that snaked through the park. Several guys were beating on empty plastic buckets and beat-up bongos. Different radios blared through the park. Squeaky was there, dancing away to the rhythm of the bongos. The warm soupy air through the park was strong with the smell of weed.

Somewhere Bonehead had found a rusty coffee can filled with dirty, scratched marbles. Sure enough, he was throwing the marbles up one at a time, whacking them with efficient power. The stick would whistle through the air and make contact with a sharp crack. Bonehead's baby squirrel was still in his pocket and seemed to enjoy the regular swing of her new mama. At least Bonehead was aiming the marbles into an old children's playground that nobody used in the day. The grass had grown over the jungle gym and lots of hypodermic needles were scattered in the trash.

Every now and then, Bonehead would look around with that look of someone who was expecting a friend any moment. Then he would hit another marble. First a whiz from his stick and then a crack. One marble sailed right over the playground. Bonehead heard a sharp *ping* as the marble hit a car.

"Hey!" came a shout from behind the overgrown jungle gym. Bonehead quietly picked up his coffee can and the box he kept his baby squirrel in. He drifted to another part of the park as the shadows from the buildings grew longer across the pathways.

Squid opened his eyes but still wasn't sure whether his eyes were open or closed. He was staring into total darkness and didn't have a clue where he was. He had slept so deeply that he felt as though he were coming up for air from twenty feet under the surface. He knew he had just had a bunch of dreams—sharp, clear dreams. Big dreams, upsetting dreams. He put his hands to his head as he felt the dreams escaping from his consciousness. But he could only remember the last part. Something about Bonehead and the fire escape. No, everyone was climbing down. Unc and Jason, Rachel and Bonehead. Others too—Larry, Molly, and Ratchet. Don Mattingly and Reggie Jackson. Maybe even Saw. Or maybe he made that part up. Something upsetting had happened. They were all climbing down. Squid was still half asleep. "Watch out! That ladder is really rusty!" he said aloud. His voice echoed against the walls in the basement and he realized he was awake. He wanted everyone to be safe. Even Ratchet and Larry.

Squid still could not remember where he was. It was not his bed. It was way too hard and way too dark. He felt as though he had been sleeping for a very long time. Slowly, his memory of all that had happened on the previous day came back, and the dream receded quietly to a back corner of his mind, like a cat. His head was still resting on the concrete ledge. He wasn't scared. His surroundings were just as dark when his eyes were opened as when they were closed.

Squid wasn't yet ready to move his arms. What came to mind again in the darkness was that man crying out, pinned to a board. It was the same man he had seen when he bowed his head and closed his eyes with Rachel. The man was cut up bad and there was blood on his face. He had cuts from his hands and feet where he had been pinned. "You know about knives," Squid whispered.

The sound of his voice echoed in the empty black room in the basement. Quietly, after another minute,

Squid realized where he was, though he still couldn't see a thing. He didn't move, trying to sort things out. What was different? He often had upsetting dreams, dreams that seemed so clear and sharp at the time, dreams that made him anxious. What was absent? It was like finally realizing the air conditioner on a nearby building has been shut off. Somehow, although he was lying in the dark in this damp, stinking basement, he didn't feel afraid. That was it. His stomach didn't hurt too much. Everything Squid did was usually because he was afraid. Most of his actions depended on that emotion. It was gone. It was like realizing a toothache wasn't there anymore.

In a physical sense, this was probably the safest he had been all day. He had gotten some sleep. Nobody knew where he was. He couldn't be betrayed. If anyone opened that screeching, grating door, he would know it and have some time to prepare. He could stay here for a long time if he wanted to, just pee in the corner of the other room and sit here. It was like his little hole where he could hibernate, if he wanted to. Squid savored the feeling of waking up from a long sleep and feeling safe.

A wisp of the dream came back to him. "Wait a minute," he said to himself. "What time is it?" He scrambled to his feet in a frenzy and hit his head on a big pipe hanging from the ceiling. "Ouch!" he spat as he felt his way to the stairway. He had to get to the third floor to see the clock in the Con Ed tower. He felt as though he had slept several hours, but what if he had slept longer than that? What if he had slept past the time to meet Rachel?

Squid ran up the stairs, forgetting about being quiet. People might be waiting for him up there, but he didn't care. He had to make sure he still had time. The door to the basement scratched against the floor as he shoved it open. He ran up the first flight of steps, almost slipping on the banister next to the missing stairs. It was night. He didn't stop to see who was smoking crack or shooting up on the second floor. He got to the third floor and rushed to the front window to see the time. Everything was still dark outside. Ten minutes until four o'clock. Squid cursed. He had slept much longer than he had planned. Still, if he rushed, he could still make it. The parking lot wasn't far away.

Squid checked the other rooms to make sure nobody was waiting to jump him. He looked in his stack of clothes to find a cleaner shirt. Some light came in the windows from the street lights below, but basically he was just feeling around and guessing which one had been worn the least. He found one. Squid patted his hair, said, "One, two, three," and shoved some gum in his mouth. There was no time to do anything else; he had to go.

As Squid ran back down the stairs, he was surprised at how lighthearted he felt. He hadn't died in the last twenty-four hours. He didn't even have one cut on him. He had been smart and brave, just like Unc had told him to be. He had had this whole new thing happen to him as he sat in the dining room of the mission house. He had been smart in finding a place to sleep. But most of all, Squid knew, he was lighthearted because he was going to see Rachel. He didn't care anymore that Jason was there. He knew in his heart he didn't have a chance with Rachel. He just wanted to be around her, to talk to her about anything, to see her blow her cheeks out and cross her blue eyes and make him laugh.

Even if she laughed a lot more at Jason's jokes than his, he didn't care. Sure, it hurt like a butcher knife under the rib, but he told himself he didn't care. He almost started liking Jason more, if he made Rachel laugh or made Rachel have more joy. Did he dream about them or something? It was a strange feeling. Liking Jason almost made him feel closer to Rachel somehow, since she liked him so much.

By the time he climbed through the window of the squat and landed on his feet, he felt light-headed. His gut and chest felt like a balloon, and goodness seemed to be expanding inside of him. No, it was more like a sunrise, like the dawn, because there wasn't any boundary to this goodness. He was actually going to see the sunrise with Rachel today. He hoped it was one with lots of colors. He liked it in the summer when the morning light looked really red through the smoggy haze. In his heart, Squid congratulated himself because he didn't want to kill Jason anymore. It didn't really matter. He was going to see Rachel.

The street in front of his squat was pretty deserted. It was a few minutes before four o'clock. A slight tinge of coolness, like morning dew, made the heat a little more bearable. The silence and the streetlights made the street seem almost like a movie set, as if all the buildings had props behind them instead of rooms. Squid stood under the streetlight and pulled out the card that Unc had left him and read it quickly: "'Today there are once more villains and saints. . . . The outlines stand out with exaggerated sharpness. Reality lays itself bare. Shakespeare's characters walk in our midst.' — Dietrich Bonhoeffer"

"Who's that guy? What's he talking about?" Squid asked aloud to nobody. This was a quote that Squid didn't get. He had to keep moving. Squid adjusted his pants. He didn't have time to change them, and he still had the bat dangling down the side of his leg. His toe felt more swollen, and he had to twist his foot a certain way when he walked, but it didn't hurt anymore than it had the previous afternoon.

Two guys Squid didn't know stood on the corner looking for customers. They looked at Squid. "Sense, sense, smoke, smoke," they said for the thousandth time that night. Their eyes locked in to Squid's. Their looks were intense and blank. They didn't know Squid. He just might be a customer.

Squid shrugged. "No money," he explained.

Even though Squid's street had been empty, people dotted the nearby avenue. Some were selling drugs, some were hanging out on stoops and drinking. Some people looked like they were heading home from parties. Squid realized that there were about just as many people out at that moment as there were at four o'clock in the afternoon. They were just different people. Junkies lined up on one corner because the drug dealer on that street wouldn't let them hang out close to the distribution point. They were specters, ghosts, with all the life sucked out of them.

Squid knew some of them. They had strange names like Turkey and Alabama and Sweetwater. Sometimes they ate at the mission. The drug dealer wouldn't let them bring big bills. They had to have the exact amount.

"You got any change for a twenty-dollar bill?" one of them asked Squid with mournful eyes as she shifted from foot to foot.

Squid walked by and turned the corner again. "Nope," he said as he passed. Steam kept coming up through the manholes. Squid was getting close to the parking lot, and things became all quiet again. Squid listened to his footsteps echo down the street and pretended he was on a movie set. He walked through the steam coming out of the manhole covers. It smelled like someone melting aluminum.

It must be about four o'clock. Maybe Rachel and Jason would be waiting for him. They would catch the bus and have a lot of time to laugh and talk. Squid got to the parking lot, but no one was there. The parking lot had nothing but a couple of old cars in it and a little light from the street. The lot had an old chain-link fence in front of it, but the gates were wide open. The adjacent buildings had no windows facing the lot.

Squid sat down on the curb then stood up again and started biting his thumbs. He was so excited. He rehearsed things he could say to Rachel as they waited to see the animals. He felt like he did on that good birthday with his mom, waiting to eat ice cream. Still no Rachel. Squid could hear car traffic several blocks away, but everything was very quiet where he stood.

Squid began to feel uncomfortable. He spoke out loud, just to steel his nerves. "I'm in a *Twilight Zone* where everyone on earth has been killed but me." Squid leaned against a fire hydrant. "And Rachel. That's why it is so quiet here." His voice sounded tiny, as if the words hadn't gotten two feet away from his mouth before they disappeared.

Squid heard the footsteps before he saw the figures. They were walking down the middle of the street, and the steam from the manholes covered their forms.

"Rachel!" Squid called out with relief. He squinted his eyes to see through the steam. It wasn't Rachel. Two people were walking toward him. One of them was carrying something in his hand. Maybe it was a large book or package. "Unc?" Squid asked. "Jason?"

The second man placed what he had in his hands on his head. It was a large sombrero. "Larry?" Squid asked and began reaching for his bat. The first man had passed over the manhole, and the second figure slowly emerged from the steam. He had a leather vest on, and the dark skin on his huge biceps gleamed as if had just put oil on them. Strapped on the leg of his camouflage pants was a knife sheath that was empty. Wrapped around his head was a black scarf. His sunglasses made his face look passive, but he forced a strange smile. It was more like an animal baring its teeth. Up this close, Squid could see the sharp-filed teeth that gave him his name.

In Saw's hand flashed the large hunting knife. Saw held it loosely, weighing it lightly with his hand. Saw moved slowly toward Squid with confidence, like an athlete who had done what he was about to do many times. Squid took a step back toward the fire hydrant, and Saw quickly moved past Squid to block any escape down the street.

Now Larry with a smaller knife was to Squid's right, and Saw was to Squid's left. Squid took another couple of steps backward toward the parking lot. *Betrayed!* roared in Squid's head as he tried to pull his little bat out of his pants. *Betrayed by Rachel and Jason, ditched by Unc, choked by Ratchet, beaten by Squeaky and Cheese.*

Squid pulled the souvenir bat out about four inches from his pants, but the twine had caught it tight. "Look, Saw," Squid said. As Squid yanked at the bat, he suddenly thought he might pee in his pants. "I know I messed up. I know I cheated you. Just give me a day or two and I'll give you back your money."

Larry smiled and edged closer to Squid. "We thought you were in the hospital, until you conveniently showed up at church for poor Peaches. We were the ones who took care of Peaches, you know. And now your friend Rachel helped us to find you. She gave us the last bit of information that we needed. It was all very easy, man."

"Rachel?" Squid twisted his pants around the bat. Uneasy feelings from his dreams rumbled back into his memory.

Larry took a step closer. "Yeah, Ratchet was able to squeeze a little info out of Unc first. It only cost us five bucks 'cause Unc was so thirsty. And this is perfect. We wanted a place so that we could take our time as we deal with you."

Squid backed up further into the lot and frantically tried to free his bat from his pants. The waist of his pants was all twisted up and the edge of the bat was pushing his pant leg out, making it look huge. Even without his sprained toe, Squid knew that Saw was much faster than he was. He couldn't make a run for it. He had a sinking feeling. He knew he was being forced back into a stupid, stupid place.

The two men kept stepping forward with their knives out. Squid backed through the open gate of the lot. It was much darker where he was standing. The streetlight didn't penetrate so well. Squid checked his exit routes. A building on each side and a chain-link fence in the back. No windows on the buildings. No one would hear him cry out.

Saw moved forward slowly like a snake whose prey is cornered. They could take their time now. Squid's legs felt paralyzed.

Squid could not get the bat out, not that it mattered anymore. It was stuck halfway out, the bottom half splaying out to the side as if he were wearing riding pants. Squid couldn't keep himself from talking. "Look, Saw, you know, I did take your hundred bucks, and I'm sorry, man. Maybe I deserve what I get. Look, I can't deny that if I had a chance I would have killed you today. But maybe not. I was just scared and that's what I do when I'm scared. It was me that was in your apartment. I don't know what I was doing. So maybe you have a right to kill me, I don't know. But look Saw, I hate knives. I just do. Could you just take my bat . . ." Once more Squid tried to extricate his Yankee bat from his twisted pants. "Could you just take my bat and beat me to death or something? Just do something to me fast. Maybe hit me in the head first and knock me out real good or something."

No emotion was showing in Saw's expression except a calm pleasure. He was taking his time, a predator with a tiny mesmerized animal. Squid was halfway to the back of the lot. Saw moved forward to grab his arm.

At that moment, Larry's sombrero flew off with a whizzing sound. A fraction of an instant later, the whizzing sound came again and cracked Larry's knife hand sharply. The knife flew to the ground with a rattle. Squid could see a little figure in the shadows taking a batter's stance. The next instant, Larry's head flew back with a whack. Something had hit him in the face. Twice in rapid succession, the whizzing sound came again even louder. Larry clapped his hands over each ear and backed away. The little figure stepped into the light and whacked Larry again straight in the face. It was Bonehead, doing the one thing Bonehead did best, using his heavy stick as a bat to hit home runs all over Larry's body.

Larry must have felt he was surrounded by fifteen thugs. Blood covered his eyes and ears. He ran out of the parking lot gate like a hunted rabbit.

Without missing a beat Bonehead moved toward Saw. Saw, like Squid, had stood stunned for the first few instants. Seeing harmless Bonehead moving with the fierce coolness of an avenging angel gave even the most seasoned fighter a moment's pause. But Saw was in a different league on the street than Larry. He moved toward Bonehead with a growl.

Bonehead took a swing at Saw's head but Saw quickly moved backward. A little squeal came from Bonehead's front pocket. Squid could see the top of Flicker's head in the light from the street. Bonehead put his stick in his left hand and scooped Flicker out of his pocket with his right hand. Keeping his eye on Saw, he crouched and put Flicker on the ground, shoving her toward Squid.

Squid crouched down on the gravel in the dark and held his stomach. He kept his eyes on Flicker but he found he couldn't move. His legs felt like dead pieces of wood. He tried to call out, but it felt as though someone were choking him. "Come on, Flicker, over here!" Squid finally found his voice. Flicker sat on the gravel, shivering, as Bonehead took another swing at Saw. The stick made a threatening whiz as it almost hit Saw's hand. Saw placed himself to face Bonehead but kept Squid in his line of vision. Saw adjusted the knife in his hand and was ready to strike. The knife flashed for a moment in the beam of the street lamp.

When the knife flashed, Squid looked around quickly for a place to hide. He felt like he was ten years old. Then he heard another tiny squeal of distress from Flicker. She took an uncertain hop toward Bonehead and stopped. "Over here!" Squid wheezed. Finally Flicker began to move toward Squid with shaking little steps. Squid got on his hands and knees and reached out his hand toward the trembling squirrel. "Come on, little thing, come over here to safety." She was almost there.

Bonehead swung for Saw's face, and Saw feinted like a boxer. Then, in a movement so fast that Squid couldn't see it, he slashed Bonehead's arm before he could come around for a second swing. Even in the dark, Squid could see black blood dripping from Bonehead's arm onto the gravel.

Flicker squealed again. Squid swallowed hard and croaked, "Here, Flicker." He fixed his eyes on the tiny squirrel, no larger than a mouse, and crawled toward her.

Saw kept his eyes on Bonehead, but with the speed of a cat he moved toward Squid who was still on all fours and had almost reached Flicker. Keeping his knife aimed at Bonehead, he gave Squid a swift sidekick to the head with his thick boot. Squid collapsed on the gravel. Using the same foot, Saw stomped his thick boot firmly on top of the shaking little squirrel, as if he were killing a cockroach. Flicker's frail body was smashed flat into the gravel.

This delay gave Bonehead a chance to move forward with an overhead swing. Squid had never seen Bonehead's face like that before. Bonehead hit Saw's knife hand below the knuckles with precision. It was a heavy blow that made a cracking sound and probably broke bones. But the blow did not dislodge the knife from Saw's hand. Saw was off balance but ably tossed the knife to his left hand while keeping his eye on Bonehead. Saw cradled his hurt hand close to his body and momentarily looked less sure of himself.

Bonehead pressed forward. With his fat stomach and a rope keeping his pants up, he looked like a dwarf next to Saw. Bonehead swung for the left hand. His stick made a zipping sound in the air. With lightning speed, Saw pulled his hand back. The stick hit the blade of the knife with a loud *ping* but did nothing.

The two stood for a moment, facing each other as still as statues. The challenge became clear: One large man who was good with a knife against one small man who was good with a stick. Squid lay stunned on the gravel, shaking his head. He touched his stinging ear where Saw had kicked him. It was wet. The place where Flicker had been was just a flat spot of fur. Squid could see dimly that the two men had started circling and sizing each other up. Surely most of the advantage was with the knife. Saw just needed to get inside the arc of the swing to be deadly. Bonehead's goal was to keep him back.

Saw lunged toward Bonehead and tried to block the swing with his right hand while driving his knife home. Bonehead stepped just as quickly to the side and swung over the arm, hitting Saw sharply above the back of the neck twice before Saw could turn around. That was it. Saw was stunned. Bonehead moved in with a crushing swing to the forearm of Saw's left hand. The stick made a sound like the crack of a whip as it hit Saw's arm. To Saw's credit, he did not drop the knife. But his reflexes were slower and Bonehead pressed his advantage. He moved in close to Saw and swung up, as if he were going for the bleachers. The stick hit squarely under Saw's jaw with a heavy crack. A home run. Saw's head jerked back and his sunglasses flew off. Squid thought he heard Saw's teeth crack. Saw's hands went slack and Bonehead, with dogged precision, struck him once again under the jaw as he went down.

Saw fell like a telephone pole, not using his hands to protect his fall. His head hit the gravel hard, and he was out cold. Squid lay on the ground, holding his ear. He was stunned, but what happened next stunned him even more.

The instant Saw hit the ground, Bonehead was on him. He kicked the hunting knife about twenty feet away. He untied the twine that was supposed to keep his pants up. Without a moment's hesitation, Bonehead grabbed Saw's wrist and twisted Saw's body over so that he was lying on his stomach. Looping Saw's wrist back behind his back, he grabbed the other arm and began tying the hands together. Quickly, efficiently, he tied Saw's hands behind his back and left a long strand dangling down toward the legs. Next Bonehead frisked Saw in a quick military fashion. He pulled a large folding knife out of his pocket and found another smaller knife in a sheath under Saw's pants on his other leg. Bonehead threw these weapons over next to the hunting knife.

Bonehead took a moment to evaluate his own cut and then kept working. He turned Saw over and began to unbuckle his large belt. Bonehead looked so small and Saw looked so huge. Saw was like a whale being rolled back and forth on the beach. Bonehead pulled Saw's pants all the way down to his ankles. Next he pulled Saw's belt out from the pants and buckled them around Saw's ankles right next to his pants. Then Bonehead pulled the strand of twine dangling from Saw's hands and tied it tight around the pants and the belt. Bonehead gave the twine a pull and Saws feet went up like a puppet moving on a string. Saw's hands and feet were now tied together behind his back.

Bonehead was not finished. He ripped the black scarf off Saw's head and pushed part of it in his mouth and tied the scarf securely at the back of Saw's head. Bonehead worked steadily and quickly, like a soldier. Or a cop.

Squid crawled over on his hands and knees to look at what was left of Flicker. Not much. A lump of smashed fur and skin in the gravel. A little blood. Squid sat on the ground with a sigh and looked over at Bonehead working so diligently on Saw. Squid touched his ear again. The blood had already started to clot.

Saw looked very different now, lying on the gravel. He still looked huge; he still looked muscular in his arms. Yet Saw looked so exposed now. Squid had never seen Saw's legs before. They looked as thin and pale as Saw's skimpy underwear. His legs weren't strong like his arms at all. They were skinny like a little kid's legs. They looked almost frail. A new emotion for Saw welled up inside of Squid's stomach, an emotion he couldn't understand.

"Don't kill him!" Squid pleaded. "Maybe he needs a doctor!" Bonehead ignored Squid. Instead, he lifted his head up and looked at the sky, as if he were listening. Was he listening for footsteps, to see if Larry might bring back some of Saw's black magic friends? Finally, very faintly, Squid heard the sound of a siren, a long way off.

Bonehead turned and looked at Squid purposefully. Bonehead said only one word. He said it clearly and with urgent authority. "Leave!"

The night had gotten stranger and stranger. Squid knew he could not help this new Bonehead who spoke with authority. Squid felt in his gut that whatever was going to happen next in this parking lot, Squid would only be a hindrance. Yesterday, Squid would have argued with Bonehead and refused to leave. He would have probably tried to kick Bonehead. But Squid made a different decision now. He obeyed.

Squid ran out of the parking lot and onto the street. Every stride was still painful and reminded him of his swollen toe. He shoved his bat back down into his pant leg so he could set a better pace. Squid ran and limped past the line of junkies, past the drug dealers, past the people sitting on the steps and drinking.

Squid got to his own street, which was still as quiet as a movie set. He climbed through the building to get back into his squat. He hit his toe hard as he landed on the floor of his building. He clenched his teeth and took in a deep breath. Limping down the hall, he climbed up the first set of stairs and hit his toe again as he maneuvered on the banister to avoid the missing steps. He favored the whole right side of his body as he walked past Chaos and others asleep on the dirty mattresses. He pushed hard on the handrail to favor his leg and make it to the third floor.

On the third floor, Squid hobbled to the back of the building and looked out the back window, the same one he looked out almost a day ago as he planned his attack on Saw. It was still completely dark outside. Squid was breathing hard. He sat and looked at nothing as he sorted out the last few hours. Squid could not believe that he was still alive. Somehow he had been saved. He thought about

Bonehead, Rachel, Jason, Unc, Larry, Saw, and Flicker. But mostly he thought about Bonehead.

Finally Squid spoke out the window into the darkness. "He is either a narc or an angel."

Slowly the rim of the sky above the tenement buildings became lighter. All kinds of city birds began their morning songs. He wondered if the sirens he heard in the distance were a part of Bonehead and Saw's story now. From the sound of them, he couldn't tell. Objects in Squid's room became more visible. A bit of light peeked in between the buildings and illuminated the wall next to Unc's bundle of blankets and books. Squid saw the three-by-five card Unc had put up the day before, the one about welcoming three angels who mean well.

Squid fumbled in his pocket and pulled out the red crayon he had found on the ground as he was hiding from Saw, the one he had used to write WRONG on the board in Saw's apartment. That was a thousand years ago. He got up and walked over to where the card was pinned on the wall. Sticking his tongue between his teeth, he started writing very forcefully the letter *I* on the card. As he wrote the letters *B* and then *E*, the paper tore. Squid kept writing along the faded plaster of the wall, each letter larger than the last—*L* then *IEVE*, as hard and as fast as he could. He couldn't remember if the *I* or the *E* came first, but he didn't care. Each letter he wrote got larger. The first letter he wrote was a half-inch tall. The last letter was four feet tall, written all the way across the wall. He ran out of crayon before the final stroke. The last little bit of crayon dropped to the floor as he worked on the final *E*.

Squid stepped back and looked as the morning sunlight made the red crayon letters glow across the faded yellow plaster. Then he walked over to his special window and squatted. He looked around one more time out of habit to make sure no one was looking.

Carefully, slowly, he took the little chip of brick off his special place. Then gently, deliberately, he removed the brick from the wall and placed it quietly on the floor. He pulled out the old envelope with the red border and opened the flap. His room was as quiet as a church. He carefully pulled out the piece of paper inside and looked at what it said.

It was the name that no one in his life now knew. No one in the squat knew it. Not Unc, not even Rachel. It was the name that he remembered his mother, on the good days, calling him when he was very young and nestled in her arms in the rocker as she sang. It was the name he read in the book at the doctor's office as a little boy. It was the name that made sense of his life. With his index finger, he delicately touched the top and both sides of each letter. He said each letter out loud and then counted. "J. One, two, three," he whispered. "A. One, two, three. K. One, two, three. E. One, two, three." Sometimes, when his mother crooned his name in a song, she even called him Jacob.

As he said the last letters on the card and the last numbers, he held the paper tenderly in his hands and looked toward the first signs of a red, red dawn. No more fighting with Bonehead or himself, at least for now. No more running from Saw. He knew he was limping on the cusp of new light. Rachel had told him about a new name. The air was no longer humid but clean and sweet. He strained forward in the dawn toward the window to listen, to hear that new name that was almost but not quite yet spoken.

ALL ROYALTIES FROM this book go to Graffiti Community Ministries, Inc., which is the service arm of the East Seventh Street Baptist Church, nicknamed Graffiti, on the Lower East Side of Manhattan. Graffiti shares the good news of Jesus Christ, provides emergency help for the homeless, offers education opportunities for children and youth, administers job development programs, and engages in Christian discipleship. If you wish to make a contribution to this ministry, send a check payable to Graffiti Community Ministries, 205 E. 7th Street, New York, NY 10009.

For more information, please call (212) 473-0044 or see our Web site at www.graffitichurch.org.